SO-AEX-931

"Two hours."

Garrett tried not to frown. Only two hours. He wanted to make them count, but he didn't know what she liked. He pointed across the street. "You've probably seen the art gallery over there, haven't you?"

Her eyes lit up. "Not the new exhibits."

He'd hit the jackpot with Kendra.

Chase? Not really. The perpetual sparkle in the kid's eyes faded, but it reappeared in an instant. "I know. You two go check out the art gallery until Kendra has to work. I'll go home and review for a test tomorrow. Garrett can meet me there, and maybe we'll shoot hoops or something."

Yesss! Two whole hours with Kendra alone—at least as alone as they could be in the middle of five gazillion people. But what did she think? He said slowly, "Sounds fun, but—"

"Great! Kendra will give you directions." Chase zoomed off.

Now what? Garrett liked problem solving that involved steel, concrete, and precise measurements. When it involved women? Not so much... especially this statuesque redhead whose brown-eyed gaze held him helpless as if he were caught in traffic again.

RACHAEL PHILLIPS

(www.rachaelwrites.com), born and raised in Indiana, is an award-winning fiction and nonfiction writer. She is the author of four Barbour biographies, a women's Bible reference guide, three novellas, and two other Heartsong books, *The Greatest Show on Earth* and *The Return of Miss Blueberry* (both set in Indiana festivals). She has contributed over 400 articles for newspapers, magazines, and collections.

Years ago, Rachael's daughter Christy wrote a fifth-grade report on Parke County's covered bridges, planting the seeds for *Kissing Bridges*. Like Kendra and Garrett, Rachael and her family checked out all thirty-one. Two decades later, she retraced their steps, savoring memories as well as the research. She hopes readers will enjoy this Parke County story as much as she enjoyed writing it.

Books by Rachael Phillips

HEARTSONG PRESENTS

HP1005—*The Greatest Show on Earth*
HP1025—*The Return of Miss Blueberry*

Kissing Bridges

Rachael Phillips

Blessings!
Rachael Phillips

Heartsong Presents

Dedicated to the hospitable people of Parke County, Indiana,
who host two million people every year at their Covered Bridge Festival.
They answered my questions, supplied valuable information,
and made me feel at home as I nosed around their picturesque county.
Special thanks, too, to my critique partners Kim Peterson and Jaci Miller,
who demonstrate what friendship and tough love are all about.
Last, but not least, unending gratitude to my husband, Steve, for his love,
encouragement, and prayers. Not to mention his grace
on my grumpy, bumpy writer days! 1 Corinthians 13:7

A note from the Author:

I love to hear from my readers! You may correspond with me by writing:

**Rachael Phillips
Author Relations
P.O. Box 9048
Buffalo, NY 14240-9048**

ISBN-13: 978-0-373-48649-6

KISSING BRIDGES

This edition issued by special arrangement with Barbour Publishing, Inc., 1810 Barbour Drive, Uhrichsville, Ohio, U.S.A.

Chapter 1

The man said he flew often, but the white knuckles of his well-groomed hands gripping the seat's armrests betrayed him.

"A little turbulence today, but not bad." Kendra Atkinson inserted a note of motherliness into her professional voice as she turned the control wheel, adjusting the ailerons on the wings to stabilize the plane. "Ladyhawk will handle the bumps. Think of them as waves on a lake when the wind kicks up."

"I've traveled across the ocean on commercial liners in terrible weather." Garrett Beal's mouth tightened. He wiped his forehead. "Flying in a small plane seems...different."

So, getting up close and personal with the sky bothers you. When they took off near Washington, DC, her dark-haired passenger's intelligent face had impressed her. She'd even glanced at his bare ring finger.

Now he stiffened with Ladyhawk's every movement.

Nothing I like better than six hundred miles with an aerophobe beside me.

How could anyone not love soaring so high, the world at his feet? Kendra swept her gaze over the panorama. One day she'd own Ladyhawk outright, and she'd spend even more time in the air.

Watching the guy sweat, though, Kendra attempted to distract him. "Mr. Beal, did you say you're an engineer?"

He nodded, scanning the sky as if looking for fighter jets.

"Going to Rose-Hulman?" Brainy types often visited the prestigious technological institute in Terre Haute.

He nodded again. "Teaching a seminar and recruiting for my company, Global Working Solutions."

For the first time since takeoff, his royal blue eyes, through designer glasses, met hers.

Oh my. She caught her breath, reminding herself to listen to his response.

"Also, the American Heritage Bridge Association commissioned me to study the area's covered bridges."

"You're going to the right place." She grinned, pleased her tactic had relaxed him somewhat. "I live in Parke County. We have thirty-one bridges, and they're all my favorites."

"I heard—"

The plane lurched; his words died. "Wind's picking up a bit." Nothing to worry about, but he looked as if she dangled him over a cliff by one foot. She adjusted their airspeed, smiling. "Looks like rain over the Appalachians. They'll be glad. They suffered a drought last summer."

Mr. Beal didn't look glad, but he didn't cling to her as if he wanted his mommy. The next hour, as a perfectly normal fall shower splatted against the windshield, he sat ramrod straight and asked her about every instrument on the panel.

Good thing I'm used to teaching while I fly. She answered patiently but wondered how long this examination would last.

"What kind of license do you hold? How much have you flown?" His "cute guy" rating dropped to near zero as he quizzed her on her qualifications.

"I've been certified since age seventeen." That was half her lifetime ago, but why divulge that? "I've logged hundreds of flying hours, some over mountains and oceans, as well as other terrain." Kendra kept her tone measured. "I also teach aviation at Indiana State University."

He still fired questions, especially when a rumble of thunder nearly sent him into spasms.

You don't know how lucky you are, Mr. Engineer. Any other pilot would have rolled the plane by now and dumped you out—she gritted her teeth—*or at least, scared you unconscious to shut you up.*

She guided the plane away from cloud caverns. As they neared their destination, Ladyhawk seemed to purr at the thought of ditching this loser, too. Glancing at his taut face, Kendra tried to scratch up a shred of sympathy. *He's not criticizing your flying. Some people just freak their first time in a small plane.*

She cheered herself as much as him with her assurance— "We're only sixty miles from Terre Haute."

"What's the weather there?"

She sighed. "Still cloudy. A little turbulent, but I don't expect any problems."

As she spoke with the airport's tower and started her descent, the guy's shoulders under the navy golf shirt slowly rose until they almost reached his earlobes.

Hey, I don't want to crash, either. She longed to say it. Instead, she focused on gaining clearance to land and the familiar routine of gently pushing in the throttle and the control wheel, monitoring airspeed and vertical indicators, as well as the altimeter. A strong crosswind made the plane buck, nearly sending her anxious passenger through the roof. But working rudder controls with her feet, she brought Ladyhawk in for a relatively smooth landing. Taxiing down the runway, she wished people were as easy to manage as planes.

Thank You, God. Thank You. Garrett exhaled as the little plane shimmied to a stop.

"We're here." The pretty pilot cut the plane's engine. The propeller's *whop-whop-whop* slowed as she turned away to mark a clipboard. But not before he caught the *hurrah!* etched in her face.

No wonder. He'd been a pain. Especially bad because he would stay in Indiana at least three weeks, and as of now, she was the only person he knew. He liked the way her long, coppery ponytail curled down her back. "Ms. Atkinson?"

"Yes?" She faced him, raised eyebrows betraying a *Now what?*

"Thanks."

Her startlingly dark eyes widened.

"I'm sorry. I didn't mean to be obnoxious. In new situations, I tend to ask lots of questions—"

A half smile, half grimace curved her generous mouth. "So I noticed."

"I'm sure I'll be more acclimated on our return flight."

Wrong thing to say. She looked as if he'd threatened her with life imprisonment. She cleared her throat. "I'm sorry your first experience aboard a small aircraft didn't work out well. If you'd prefer a different pilot, I won't take that as an insult."

She didn't sound offended. She sounded eager to get rid of him.

"No, no, I was more than satisfied with our flight." Panic welled up at the thought of navigating rain and lightning in another toy plane without her keen eyes on the instruments, her capable freckled hands on the controls—hands without a ring....

"If that's what you want."

"That's what I want."

"All right." She threw open her door and jumped from the plane. He grabbed his briefcase and baggage, overjoyed to escape its cockpit, yet reluctant to walk to the terminal.

He couldn't take his eyes off her. She seemed to have forgotten him completely, patting her plane's wing as if it were her child before securing it with cables. The long-absent sun, peeking from behind a cloud, playfully reached for the woman's hair, its rays fooling with her thick waves. Back in DC, aghast at the tiny plane, he hadn't noticed her height. He measured six feet four inches in his socks, and she probably wouldn't have to look up to him much. He liked dating taller women. He didn't have to walk at snail's pace when they went out, his neck didn't ache from constantly looking down, and they were easier to kiss.

Kiss? First, he didn't even know her. Second, she'd also find it easier to slug him!

"Do you need directions to the terminal?" She stood by her plane, arms folded.

She'd caught him staring.

"That's it over there, right?" He felt dumb for the hundredth time that day.

She nodded, that captivating smile-grimace crossing her face before she turned and walked away.

He paused long enough for her to disappear into the hangar. Part of him wished he had followed.

Forget it, Beal. If you did, she might smack you. Entering the terminal, he summoned his mental planner to rescue him from the weird, warm fog that clouded his methodical brain. *Call contact to confirm arrival. Pick up rental car. Go to hotel. Finalize PowerPoint details for seminar.*

He pulled out his smartphone and scanned it. The comforting confines of his life cooled the chaos of his journey somewhat. Nevertheless, he wished he'd dreamed up some excuse to take a picture of the pilot stroking her plane's wingtip, her professional mask gone, her face vulnerable. He wouldn't see her again until he left for DC.

You didn't come here to meet women. The mental memo directed his thoughts past the pilot, even past the seminar, recruiting work, and covered bridge studies. Only he and God knew the real reason he'd maneuvered job and schedule to spend time in Indiana, a place he'd never visited in his life.

Please help me, Lord. I'm not sure where to start.

Chapter 2

Wind speeds registering on the instruments in the Beechcraft King Air 200's cockpit rose to dangerous levels, forecasting an imminent tropical depression. Kendra scrutinized her student's every move from behind, recording updates, rating reactions.

Natalie Brown, her short multihighlighted hair covered with a bandanna, leaned forward, jaw set, her birdlike eyes scanning the changing data. The tiny aviation student, radioing the control tower appropriately, handled each step with confidence, landing almost as well as Kendra would have.

"Good job." She high-fived Natalie.

"Man, I love this simulator." The student rose from her seat, grinning. "Great experience. I almost expect to find palm trees and ocean outside instead of red maples and cornfields."

"One nasty storm, but you aced it." Kendra left the lab with Natalie. "Keep practicing, and you'll be more than ready to fly in the Bahamas during spring break training."

They exited the Myers Technology Center through its imposing steel and glass lobby out to the rest of the Indiana State University campus. *Mmm.* The early evening air tasted crisp and delicious as the apples from her tree. Nothing better than Indiana in the fall.

She loved her students, too—most of them, anyway. As she listened to Natalie chatter, Kendra hoped airline companies wouldn't bypass her considerable skill because of her diminutive appearance.

"Want to grab a latte?" Natalie appeared ready to celebrate her success.

"I'd love to, but I'm picking up Chase at Rose-Hulman." Kendra's younger brother had opened a space in his schedule to spend with her. She'd put aside plans to work on the unfinished upstairs of her cabin.

Kendra planned to enjoy every minute of this brother-sister night, because a nagging inner voice whispered their days together might be numbered.

"Excellent presentations, Garrett. The civil engineering students in particular benefited from your classes."

Garrett warmed to the Rose-Hulman professor's words. "I enjoyed the discussion times afterward. Congratulations on your exceptional students."

In the parking lot, he recalled his informal interviews with Clement, Saunders, and Atkinson. All three asked probing questions he didn't expect from undergrads. No wonder Global Working Solutions wanted them.

Now, after two stimulating days, he looked forward to a quiet evening in a small town. Rockville, thirty miles north, was located in the heart of covered-bridge country.

Later he might take a short run to the edge of town, where he could watch a limitless sunset across endless fields, see the stars appear, and feel close to God—the beginning of a spiritual pilgrimage he'd dreamed about for months.

The first surprise: bumper-to-bumper traffic the entire way. Yes, he lived with that plague on Washington, DC's Beltway, but a thirty-mile string of cars and trucks from Terre Haute to Rockville, Indiana?

He thought about taking a different route per his GPS, but its malfunctions had led him to dead ends lately. The forested terrain surrounding the highway looked surprisingly rugged. No way did he want to get lost in the middle of nowhere at night.

By the time he reached Rockville, Garrett gave thanks for the audio book that prevented him from committing road-rage homicide. As he edged his rental car along the town's outskirts, he checked the itinerary his secretary had given him.

The Snuggle Bears Inn.

Oookay.

Thankfully, the bed-and-breakfast was located right off this street. All Garrett wanted was a quiet room, a bed onto which he could flop, and a wide-screen TV to drain the tension.

More surprises. Booths lined this main drag, lights and neon signs casting a kaleidoscope glow over crowds of people. Obviously, he'd chosen the weekend when this town celebrated its annual tractor sale or something.

He turned at a quaint sign that pointed to the inn. The white gabled house, with its large front porch and stone chimney, looked homey, the template for Hallmark movie sets. He wheeled his suitcase onto the porch past dried cornstalks, pumpkins, and gourds, past wicker rocking chairs, one of which held teddy bears dressed in overalls and gingham.

When he rang the church-chime doorbell, the heavy wooden door opened. An elderly, doll-sized woman said, "Mr. Beal? I'm Esther Kincaid. Come in. You must be about worn out." She pointed to a nearby coffee bar and a plate of breads. "Help yourself. I'll fetch your key."

Her grandmotherly fussing tasted almost as wonderful as the moist pumpkin bread. He had to remind himself not to wolf down the whole plateful.

He set his decaf on a table and dropped onto a love seat in the old-fashioned front parlor. It resembled his Aunt Clara's cluttered living room. More teddy bears occupied the chairs. Still, if tomorrow's breakfast tasted this good, he could live with the zoo.

Mrs. Kincaid bustled in, a large key in her hand. "Your room is on the second floor, the bridal suite. That's all we had left when your secretary called."

Bridal suite? He shrugged. So what if other guests wondered about his absent bride.

She recited the inn's breakfast hours. "We pride ourselves on our homemade cinnamon rolls."

He hauled his suitcase up the curved stairway. He inserted the key in the wooden door with the crystal doorknob, yanked his suitcase inside, and flicked on the light. He halted. Dozens of eyes scrutinized him.

Teddy bears. Brown ones, black ones, tan ones, all wearing wedding dresses and little black tuxes, held bouquets, parasols, and pink hearts.

No. The big bed, with its white quilt and ruffled teddy-bear cushions, was *heart* shaped. He gripped his pounding temples, wondering if he was dreaming a storybook nightmare.

Teddy bears sat in the chairs. Pictures of them stared from the walls. Teddy bear snow globes, music boxes, and figurines everywhere. *Everywhere*, even peering from greenery arranged around the hot tub.

With a groan, he switched off the light and fell across the bed, shoving pillows and the furry little intruders over the edge.

Kendra tried to rate the best smells in the world. The fragrance of bread baking in her log cabin home. Roses that once bloomed in Grandma's yard. Smoke curling from this bonfire on her forested acres, shared with Chase.

He thrust his long hot dog fork into a flame, burning marshmallows to a crisp.

He blew them out and scooped off the hot, gooey treat. "Want me to roast you more?"

"No thanks." Stuffed after their hot dog and s'more feast, she'd hit her limit. They seemed to have reached their limit on talk, too. They'd already told ghost stories, one scary enough to make Kendra check over her shoulder as she visited the woodpile. Chase picked his guitar, and they'd sung silly church camp songs from years before.

Now a silence, deep and sweet as the forest, surrounded her, broken only by mellow chords from his guitar. The firelight illuminated the undersides of golden sassafras and maple leaves above, seemingly quilted on the velvet blanket of a sky.

She savored the cathedral-like quiet—one big reason she'd bought this land several years before and began the long, hard work of building the cabin. Not easy—nothing had proved easy for her and Chase—but God had been good.

His fingers halted after "Amazing Grace."

"Kendra, have you ever asked God why He put you here?"

"No, I guess not." She lifted her gaze to the glittering sky. "I always figured He knew what He was doing, though."

"I'd like to know."

"We'd all like to know a lot of things. But God hasn't sent me any e-mails lately."

"Me, either." A grin spread across his face and then waned to a thoughtful smile. "None of the engineering internships that have accepted me really resonate, you know what I mean?"

"No…I've always wanted to fly. The whole week after Grandpa first took me to an air show, I flapped my arms and tried to take off." She laughed, remembering. "Later, I went with my gut and followed what I love. Now, with Dave selling his share in Ladyhawk, Terry and I share her, fifty-fifty. I'm one step closer to owning her outright."

Chase kidded, "Some women daydream about guys. You dream about that plane."

She made a face. "Blame Grandpa. He encouraged me to fly."

"Yeah, he did." Chase threw twigs onto the coals and watched them burst into flame, his face growing serious. "What would we have done without Grandpa and Grandma?"

"Probably crashed and burned." She didn't want to think about their long-absent father, their mother, who now called them from the East Coast once in a blue moon. "Grandma and

Grandpa made a home for us here in Parke County. I guess that's why I love it so much."

"You want to stay here forever, don't you?"

"Of course." Though his question dropped her heart to her ankles, she tried to sound natural. "It's great for both of us. Indiana State for me. Rose-Hulman for you. I wish you'd think about their graduate school. You said they'd eventually like you to teach."

"Rose-Hulman is awesome. But I'm sensing I need to do something else for a while, go somewhere else."

She'd purchased extra land with him in mind. He sat on a stump, squarely in the middle of what she hoped would one day be his living room.

Why do you want to leave?

He patted her shoulder awkwardly. "Don't worry. I haven't made any decisions yet. I just wanted you to know what's on my mind."

She tried to appreciate the courtesy he paid her, but she couldn't help asking, "How long have you been thinking this way?"

"I've been praying about it for months." Chase poked the fire. "And lately, recruiters have been visiting Rose-Hulman."

Aha! "Some of those people can make a job from Hades sound like a call from heaven."

He fidgeted then forked more marshmallows. "One guy from Washington, DC, made a lot of sense. He interviewed me later and seemed interested in me."

"How about the internships in Indianapolis? And Chicago?" At least, he could stay in the Midwest... .

Washington, DC. Garrett Beal's face popped up in her mind like an annoying ad. Didn't he say he'd be recruiting at Rose-Hulman? Kendra scowled.

She tried to herd her thoughts toward a more Christian vein. She managed to backtrack to fun time with Chase.

But deep down, she wished she'd dumped Garrett Beal out of the plane when she'd had the chance.

Chapter 3

Garrett's bucket list did not include sleeping on a heart-shaped bed with a roomful of stuffed animals. Still, he felt rested. The bubbling comfort of the hot tub, regardless of decor, relaxed him even more. The fragrance of sweet rolls floating up to his room resurrected him. Hurrying down the stairs, he made a beeline for the busy breakfast area.

His hostess introduced him to a slightly taller clone, her sister, Emily. "By the way, we're both 'Miss,'" Esther gently informed him. They served hot, cinnamony masterpieces, creamy icing melting down fluffy sides.

Miss Esther offered him coffee. "Perhaps you did not expect the Covered Bridge Festival during your stay?"

"Is that what's going on?"

"A very busy time for our entire county, but a fun one." Despite his protests, Miss Emily pressed a second roll upon him. "Each small town celebrates in its own unique way. Are you interested in covered bridges?"

"I'm planning to visit them all." He checked his smartphone. "I see three are located about a mile away."

"At Billie Creek." Miss Esther zipped past with pitchers of juice.

"You won't want to miss the goings-on at the town square." Miss Emily zoomed the opposite direction. "You can see the courthouse from our porch."

He grinned at their tag-team PR. "Thanks. I might do that."

Reluctantly Garrett refused another roll and headed outside. Sure enough, a tall limestone tower with a cupola and clock caught his eye. Using it as a reference point, he walked downtown. The nineteenth-century courthouse was flanked by long red-and-white-striped tents, which appeared to house vendors. He'd seen plenty of festival booths last night, but this morning little wooden stands crowded much of the square. Hundreds upon hundreds of people wandered the block. Miss Esther had described this time of year as "busy." An understatement. He'd return around lunchtime, when an empty stomach could appreciate a thousand tempting smells.

Several festivalgoers, armed with coffee and shopping bags, smiled as he passed. More greeted him as he walked past booths and garage sales on his route to the bridges. He felt as if he'd encountered a long-lost, if gigantic, family reunion. Did these friendly people somehow sense he and his family were rooted deep in this Hoosier soil?

The sight of Beeson Bridge quickening his steps, he crossed Billie Creek near the highway. It had been constructed Burr arch style, with heavy yellow poplar trusses angled from both ends of the bridge toward the center. The whole thing was spanned by a single large arch on each side, anchored to abutments of native sandstone. The other two, Billie Creek Bridge and Leatherwood Station Bridge, presented a similar style, though both stretched longer. Only Billie Creek, the oldest, constructed in1895, was still used for vehicular traffic.

All the builders painted Cross this bridge at a walk over each entrance because the impact of horses' trotting hooves weakened the plank floors.

Garrett thumped along the shadowy interiors. Could someone from his family have walked these bridges?

Garrett also thought of the men whose saws, axes, and sweat built these bridges more than a hundred years before. He'd designed bridges that spanned rivers much bigger than Billie Creek, but the muscles of those long-ago men and horses had accomplished near miracles that linked communities. He felt like doffing his baseball cap to them.

Exploring, measuring and taking notes, plus the walk back to Rockville, filled up his morning. After he visited a few of the town square's food booths, he looked forward to spending an afternoon on the inn's big front porch, reading pages he'd copied from Elijah Beal's journal.

Kendra and her friend Sarah wandered among the circus-like tents and rows of wooden booths everybody called "shacks."

"Never changes, does it?" Sarah stopped at one to look at pottery.

"You miss us, and you know it," Kendra teased. "Otherwise, you wouldn't show up every year for the festival."

"I miss you, especially."

"We had fun as kids, didn't we?" Kendra tasted bittersweet memories. "You could move back."

"I've thought about it." Sarah picked up a pot swirled with blues and browns. "But God has called me to help kids in Indy."

Her friend taught special education in the Indianapolis public school system. How did she do that day after day? Kendra hugged Sarah. "You're amazing, you know that? So generous."

Sarah flipped her blond hair away from her face. "You try to pretend you aren't. All those flights you make for charity, the stuff you transport to missionaries. You've even flown parents to Terre Haute for free when their students were hospitalized—"

"Okay, okay." Kendra turned her attention back to the pottery. "Let's do some serious shopping."

"Right. I wouldn't want to disappoint Landon by showing up this evening with nothing." Sarah shuddered in mock horror.

Kendra chuckled. Sarah's sweet but frugal husband probably would faint.

Sarah wanted to visit a booth that featured handmade wooden shelves, keepsake boxes, and Christmas ornaments. After they left, she whispered, "I'm spoiled. The ones you make are so much better."

"You're prejudiced." Pleased, nevertheless, Kendra vowed to do more woodworking for the next festival. This past year she'd poured most of her spare time into working on her cabin's upper story.

They shopped for hours, not stopping for a true lunch. Who needed it, what with the crullers St. Joseph Catholic Church always offered, homemade cobbler from the Chamber of Commerce shack, and ice cream served by the Boy Scouts?

Midafternoon they relaxed a little before Kendra started her volunteer shift at the info shack. Despite Sarah's taking her earlier purchases to her car, she'd loaded up again with pear and pumpkin butter for Christmas gifts.

They exchanged a fervent, lumpy hug.

"Come and see me," Sarah said.

"I will." Kendra knew their busy lives probably would keep them apart again for months.

Walking to the info shack, she already missed Sarah. Kendra loved her church family. She enjoyed friendships with her ISU colleagues, but nobody had ever taken Sarah's place.

She entered the shack, greeted the other volunteers, and perched on a stool by a window.

"Welcome to Rockville. May I help you?" Kendra would say it a hundred times, but she didn't mind. The bewildered-looking elderly couple needed someone to clarify the map they held. She greeted most of Rockville, sharing the marryin' and buryin' news.

Although Kendra found airports the best place to people watch, the Covered Bridge Festival, with two million visitors, provided plenty of entertainment. Women scanned booths with calculator eyes, martyred husbands hauling their purchases. Families pushed strollers, their little ones wearing floppy hats and smeared-ice-cream smiles. Blue-jeaned teens with purple and pink hair strung like happy, gaudy chains across the sidewalks.

"Kendra, dear." The gleam in the plump woman's eye—and the moniker *dear*—put Kendra on red alert.

Blind date! Blind date! She could almost see an emergency light rotating on Mrs. Toggle's gray head.

"You're looking lovely, as usual, dear. Do you have plans for—"

"Yes, I'm afraid my weekend is full." *Drywalling my stairway doesn't sound like much fun, but I'd rather eat dust than waste another chunk of my life with Mr. Wrong.*

"I was hoping you might show my nephew from Poughkeepsie around the festival next week—"

Ack! Why did the festival have to last so long? "Mrs. Toggle, I have to—"

"Roger is a wonderful young man. I know your blessed grandma would have loved him." Mrs. Toggle dabbed her eyes.

Kendra's heart melted, yet her fists clenched. She and the woman, Grandma's lifelong friend, had shared deep grief at her death. But why did Mrs. Toggle feel God had assigned her the role of Kendra's personal matchmaker?

"When I told Roger about your flying, he said he'd love to meet you. He's in the army, just returned from overseas." *The boy has served his country. How could you shun your patriotic duty?* said Mrs. Toggle's teary gaze.

I may as well wave the white flag. "I signed up to work here over the weekend. But I could show him around Thursday evening—"

"Roger will love it!" Tears evaporated, Mrs. Toggle clasped her many-ringed hands. "I'll have him call you after he arrives Wednesday."

For a heavy woman, Mrs. Toggle moved fast, blending into the passing crowd before Kendra could recant.

Roger. She tried the name on her tongue, like a new brand of cough medicine. He sounded older than her. Much older.

Trying to shake the image of a cane-wielding, male Mrs. Toggle, she waved good-bye to the volunteer who replaced her. A blasted blind date. She deserved fried food. Kendra followed her heart and stomach to a nearby booth, where they served her favorite golden, plate-sized tenderloin sandwiches.

Mmm. She felt better already.

Wandering down the street after eating, she spotted a blue and white scrolled sign that quickened her steps: Hort's Heavenly Elephant Ears.

"Hello, Red Wonder!" The elderly man with twinkling dark eyes waved from the window of a little white stand. He buttered large, flat, golden brown treats he'd just taken from the deep fryer. "I can see you need an elephant ear."

"Sure do, Hort." She grinned at hearing the childhood nickname. "But I'll take my turn, like you taught us when we were kids."

She moved to the back of an eager line of customers. An elderly couple worked with Hort to send the elephant ears out almost as fast as new customers gathered. Soon she stepped to the head of the line.

"Here you go, Kendra." Hort pushed a steaming pastry toward her. "Enjoy!"

"I sure will." She inhaled the luscious fragrance and promised herself another one during her blind date. If it really stunk, she'd eat two.

"Wish I could talk now, but you know the weekends." He kept the line moving. "Can you come back sometime during the week? Then we can sit a spell."

"Will do." She carried the elephant ear to a small table under Hort's awning. This yummy splurge would energize her to work a little on her stairway tonight.

She startled and nearly dropped it. A tall, blue-jeaned figure strode down the sidewalk, roasted ears of corn in one hand, a near-bucket of cola in the other. His sky-colored eyes scanned the area for a place to sit.

Garrett Beal.

Clutching her elephant ear, she backed to the corner of the awning. *If he sees me, he'll ask me questions.*

She sneaked away toward the courthouse but realized Hort saw her escape. He missed nothing that happened around his stand.

But why concern herself with Hort? Mrs. Toggle, who probably already had reserved the church for her and Roger's wedding, no doubt watched with binoculars.

Kendra found a small grassy area by a scarlet bush where she could eat her elephant ear in peace. As she munched its cinnamon-sugary goodness, her face heated.

Red Wonder. Right now, the name described her face to a tee. Why had she overreacted? Behaved like a twelve-year-old.

He's trying to recruit Chase, she defended herself. *He's trying to talk my brother into moving to Washington, DC.*

At the thought, a fresh flush of anger swept over her.

She didn't care if he had a right to attend the festival like anyone else. She didn't care that he appeared to be alone, a stranger she would ordinarily welcome.

You're after my baby brother, and I'm going to stop you.

Chapter 4

Two tall redheads sat near the front of the white-walled, red-carpeted church, one with mop-like curls, the other wearing a long, coppery ponytail. Garrett, who had just slipped into a polished wooden pew in the back during an organ prelude, tried not to crane his neck.

Could that be the pilot who had brought him to Indiana? He wished he could see her face, even her profile. Instead, she spoke to the people in front of her and then bowed her head.

She was praying before the service? Garrett guiltily dropped his chin. After all, he'd come to this church first and foremost to worship Christ. He thanked God for bringing him this far on his spiritual pilgrimage.

The choir opened with a simple, moving anthem. Garrett, who knew some contemporary worship songs, buried his head in the red hymnbook, trying to follow the congregation. Their songs included "And Can It Be," which he didn't know but recognized from his research as written by Charles Wesley.

"Amazing Love, how can it be, that Thou, my God, shouldst die for me?"

He stumbled a little over the King James-style language, but the words consumed him. Perhaps the ancestors of this congregation had sung these words when Elijah Beal preached.

The same God they worshipped gave this pastor the rich truth he now shared. "Hear, O Israel: The Lord our God, the Lord is one. Love the Lord your God with all your heart and with all your soul and with all your strength."

The same God had brought Garrett here, too.

Great sermon, but a little long. Kendra rose with the congregation for the benediction. Her muscles stretched, glad for movement, and though Pastor Jeff's words had inspired her, the beautiful day outside beckoned. She couldn't wait to hit the festival again. "Where do you want to eat today, Chase?"

"Want to go to the Bridgeton festival for some sati babi?" He licked his lips.

They wandered to the back of the sanctuary. "I love Filipino, too, but the traffic's too heavy to risk going there. I have to be back in time to work at the info booth—"

"Hey." He was looking past her. "There's that exec from Washington, DC." He charged down the middle aisle like a kindergartener.

Unless the guy had a twin, it was…Garrett Beal. Kendra wanted to close her eyes, to shut out the awesome Sunday morning picture he made standing in the church vestibule. But his cerulean gaze through the trendy glasses made that impossible.

Chase shook the man's hand as if he were a long-lost relative. He called, "Kendra, I want you to meet someone."

Gluing on a cordial smile, she exited the sanctuary and joined them.

The guy extended his hand. "Actually, I've already had that privilege."

"Seriously?" Chase gave Kendra an accusing look. "You didn't tell me you met Garrett."

She brushed his fingers in an "acquaintance" handshake. "I flew him here from Washington."

"I had no idea Chase was your brother. But seeing you together, the resemblance is hard to miss."

"I'm the better-looking kid in the family, but she's not bad." Chase summoned his evil-genius grin.

Garrett chuckled, a deep, masculine sound.

Now what was she supposed to say? "Pleased to meet you"? She'd already met him, and she wasn't pleased, especially since Chase stared at the man as if he were the ultimate engineering guru.

Her brother snapped his fingers. "Hey, do you have plans for lunch? If not, eat with us. We're going to grab something at the festival."

"I'd like that." Garrett the Guru's voice rose slightly, as if asking a question. He looked at Kendra.

Chase turned to her, too, eager as an Irish setter.

Did a wistful smile tug at Garrett's perfect lips?

The hospitable Hoosier in her couldn't let someone stay lonely on a Sunday afternoon. She tried to inject warmth into her voice. "Sure. Please join us."

Garrett couldn't have asked for a more enthusiastic festival guide—especially when it came to lunch.

Chase waved a hand at the stands as if he owned them. "I'm sure you've eaten in awesome restaurants in Washington, but you won't find better food anywhere. What do you like? Smoked pork chops? Barbecue chicken? Steak or walleye sandwiches? Homemade pork rinds?"

Garrett shook his head. "Actually, I'm a vegetarian."

Kendra, who had said little as they'd braved the town-square crowds, shot him a look he didn't know how to interpret. Maybe, *Are you one of those tofu-eating cholesterol phobes who faints at the sight of steak sauce?*

Chase didn't miss a beat. "No problem. The Little League always sells potatoes. There's a Chinese booth somewhere around here." He brightened. "Or I could take you to one of my favorite places. They make incredible fried veggies, but I love their fried pickles and their fried candy bars, too."

Garrett could feel his trainer shudder all the way from DC. He'd counted on a spiritual adventure, not a gastrointestinal one. Did even the drinking water contain lard? "Um, anybody around here serve salad?"

"The restaurants do." Chase's forehead wrinkled. "But with all this amazing festival food, do you really want to eat that green stuff while you're here?"

"You might wait awhile before you're served." Kendra regarded him with those dark, dark eyes.

They'd kindly included him, and he didn't want to delay their plans. Plus, the delicious aromas that wafted through the church's windows had done their job. "I'm sure we're all too hungry for that. Lead me to the fried veggies." *But not the fried pickles.*

They sat on a wall that edged the courthouse. The steaming batter-dipped mushrooms, cauliflower, and broccoli definitely moved onto his favorites list. Chase's nonstop conversation filled the emptiness of what would have been another meal alone. He also liked sneaking glances at Kendra. After disappearing a short while, she brought back luscious, cinnamony baked apples for all, apples grown at a friend's orchard.

Kendra not only knew the origins of even the apples in Rockville, she introduced him to at least twenty people of every age, size, and shape. He couldn't picture the same thing happening in DC.

Chase stuffed the last bite of apple into his mouth. "Garrett, how about dessert?"

"I thought the apples were dessert."

Chase gave him a pitying look. "In my omnipotent official festival book, they rate as a side. I mean *real* dessert."

Kendra said, "I think he's telling you he's full, Chase. Not everybody visits every booth in every town the way you do." She turned and glanced at the courthouse clock.

"How long before your shift, Sis?"

"Two hours."

Garrett tried not to frown. Only two hours. He wanted to make them count, but he didn't know what she liked. He pointed across the street. "You've probably seen the art gallery over there, haven't you?"

Her eyes lit up. "Not the new exhibits."

He'd hit the jackpot with Kendra.

Chase? Not really. The perpetual sparkle in the kid's eyes faded, but it reappeared in an instant. "I know. You two go check out the art gallery until Kendra has to work. I'll go home and review for a test tomorrow. Garrett can meet me there, and maybe we'll shoot hoops or something."

Yesss! Two whole hours with Kendra alone—at least as alone as they could be in the middle of five gazillion people. But what did she think? He said slowly, "Sounds fun, but—"

"Great! Kendra will give you directions." Chase zoomed off.

Now what? Garrett liked problem solving that involved steel, concrete, and precise measurements. When it involved women? Not so much…especially this statuesque redhead whose brown-eyed gaze held him helpless as if he were caught in traffic again.

"If you have other plans, please feel free to do whatever you like." Kendra forced a smile to her lips. *Chase, you are so on my blacklist—*

"I'd enjoy seeing the art gallery." His words sped up from a walk to a jog. "Also, I don't know much about the festival or the area. I'd appreciate it if you'd show me around."

So, this guy not only wanted to recruit her brother, he also wanted a free tour guide? A real opportunist. Yet at the entreaty in his voice, her heartbeat yammered in her ears. "I—I guess I haven't made time to see the art gallery lately."

What was the matter with her? She could visit it next week.

"I really would like to see it…with you."

Her heart stopped. "All right."

When it started beating again, she couldn't say. But her resuscitation had something to do with the power of those sapphire eyes.

Chapter 5

Kendra had given him her cell number yesterday, so why did he hesitate?

Garrett munched the Chinese stir-fry he'd bought from a booth. Sipping iced tea and watching the smaller, but still plentiful, Monday crowd fill the town square, he analyzed his near date with Kendra step-by-step. He knew better than to attempt to figure out women, but in this case, he couldn't help but try.

She'd seemed to enjoy their time together at the art gallery, where they'd viewed mostly paintings associated with the covered bridges in every season. He told her about the research he was conducting about the bridges, and she seemed pleased. Kendra explained all sorts of details connected with various exhibits, glowing with pride as if she were introducing members of her family. He'd never met anyone quite so attached to her home, but her magic rubbed off on him—in more ways than one.

At the end of their tour, though, when he asked for her number, that odd smile-grimace had appeared on her face again. After a moment she gave it, but with a quick " bye," she strode to the information shack as if she could happily never see him again.

The problem? He wanted to see her. Very much.

Would she distract him from his spiritual goals?

Garrett had pondered that during his prayer time this morning on the inn's front porch. He'd already fallen under the spell of those sparkling dark eyes, and he knew it. The distance that separated their homes and lives? He wouldn't deal with that. He did believe her perspective of this land of his ancestors would speak volumes more to him than if he tried to explore it on his own.

Garrett pulled out his phone. *With Your help, I'll keep my priorities straight, Lord.*

As the phone rang, he chuckled ruefully. Priorities? If Kendra imprisoned him in eternal voice mail, he wouldn't have to worry.

"Want to see more covered bridges on the way to Bridgeton?" Kendra accelerated as they left Rockville's city limits.

"Awesome."

At his incredible grin, she couldn't help smiling. *I can't believe I'm doing this.*

He continued, "You're talking about the Neet, McAllister, Crooks, and Nevins bridges, right?

"You've done your research."

He caught her glance and held it. "I'm looking forward to knowing even more."

He placed an oh-so-slight emphasis on the word *more*. She could and should keep her eyes on the road, winding through the gold and scarlet patchwork forests, but his words stuck to her like pretty purple thistles.

When she took a turn a little sharper than necessary onto a gravel road, he stiffened.

She said, "I hope you don't mind if we take the scenic route. Less traffic and more fun."

"I came to see Parke County, not stay on the beaten paths."

She couldn't help liking that strong, square chin he raised. *Why so interested in Parke County?* No doubt, the covered bridges might attract an engineer's interest for a weekend, but she wouldn't fly Garrett back to Washington for another two and a half weeks. Maybe his relatives lived nearby?

She might learn more if she encouraged him to talk. "Did you guys have fun yesterday?"

"Oh yeah. I won all three games in *the* One-on-One Basketball Championship of the World."

"Chase didn't tell me that." No wonder. He hated losing at anything.

"I didn't tell him I played basketball two years during college." Garrett grinned. "Mostly warmed the bench, but I played in a game or two."

"Chase and I played on our high school teams," Kendra said, and they talked hoops until they reached Crooks Bridge. She hadn't learned much. But then, why all this conjecture? He wanted Chase to go to Washington. She didn't need to know his other plans... .

"Are you sure we can drive through this covered bridge?" He pointed to the nearby, newer bridge spanning Little Raccoon Creek's rushing waters.

"Yes, Crooks Bridge is still open—if you want to use it."

"Can we drive through and then stop?"

"Sure." She pulled the Jeep into the dim interior of the barn-red and white structure with a tin roof.

"This is an oldie." Garrett's voice dropped to an almost reverent tone. "Built somewhere between 1856 and 1860, never designed to hold vehicles like this, yet still in operation."

When she parked along the country road, he leaped out of the Jeep. "I can't believe the timbers those guys felled to build these things. How did they install the bridge without hydraulics? How did they ever cut the stone for the abutment? This bridge has survived a lot—"

"Floods and rerouting of the creek." Kendra nodded. "It

sat over a dry creek bed for some time. Then the bridge was moved here—before a road even existed."

"Obviously a government project." Garrett grinned.

She laughed, too. "Sometimes people still call it the 'Lost Bridge.' "

"How do you know all this?"

"Remember, I work at the information booth. Plus, when I was in fifth grade, we studied the bridges. My interest in local history grew, and now I'm a Parke County buff."

They walked back through the structure, Garrett flicking a flashlight, muttering about struts, angles, and bolts, making notes on his smartphone. She strolled beside him and watched him examine and measure.

Red-winged blackbirds called to each other as Garrett edged down through brown grasses toward the bottom. "Water's running fast. Sure wouldn't want to drive my car through it."

"We've had a wet fall." She followed, peering around him.

He glanced at the trees, the golden rustling corn and soybean fields. "So quiet. What would it be like to live out here in the middle of—"

"In the middle of nowhere?" What did he expect, a mall?

"In the middle of such a peaceful, spacious place."

His mild tone and raised eyebrows brought the heat back to her cheeks. "I'm sorry. Sometimes I grow defensive when self-appointed critics don't see this part of the country the way I see it."

"Not all of us city slickers are bent on criticism."

She'd stereotyped him. She, who hated stereotypes. "I really do apologize." She reached a hand in what she hoped was a shake-only pose. "The country mouse proposes a truce with the city mouse."

Extending his, he gave her a quizzical look. "I didn't know we were at war, but sounds like a good idea."

She couldn't say anything right to this man. Good. After all, he was trying to talk Chase into moving to Washington. Her heart defied him with eloquent speeches.

"Maybe we could move on to the McAllister Bridge?" His question broke her reverie. He looked down at their hands.

She still gripped his fingers. "Uh, sure." Kendra dropped his hand and hurried to the Jeep.

Garrett had caught the look in her eyes, her face, before he reminded her to release his hand. *You may not want to like me, Kendra, but you do.*

Exactly why she scorned urban dwellers remained a mystery, but for now, he decided not to ask questions. They exchanged chitchat as they visited the McAllister, Neet, and Nevins Bridges, neither mentioning the hand-holding incident, though Garrett replayed it several times in his mind.

As they approached the small town of Bridgeton, the sight of its bridge momentarily diverted his attention from Kendra.

"That's the first Burr arch two-span I've seen." Garrett pointed at the long structure stretching majestically above a dam's noisy waterfall. "Has to be around two hundred fifty feet. That's not the original, right?"

"The original was built back around the Civil War." Kendra turned into a parking lot by a large stream splashing over mossy, flat rocks. "Arson destroyed it a few years ago, but the community rebuilt it, the only new covered bridge in Parke County."

They hiked across the crowded parking lot. Walking across the bridge, he watched light reach through its occasional windows to grasp at her hair as if it were red gold.

Oh yeah, he also observed the structure of the bridge.

"See that mill?" She pointed as they exited. "They claim it's the oldest continually in operation in Indiana—one hundred eighty years of splitting lumber or grinding grain. At one time, it did both. Not sure how the flour tasted then." She grinned. "Today it's strictly a gristmill. Their stone-ground mixes make some of the best breads I've ever tasted. Want to go inside?"

She ducked into the tin-roofed, barn-red building before he could answer. He did the math and realized Elijah Beal might have ridden past this mill when he visited Bridgeton to preach. Maybe he even ate corn pone baked from grain ground here.

Garrett heard the grinding sound and felt the millstones' vibration through his feet before he saw the red-and-white barrel that encased them. The big raftered room held dozens of customers who scrutinized rows of bags of wheat, oat, and rye flour; yellow, white, blue, red and even purple cornmeal. Kendra bought several mixes, throwing them into her backpack. The friendly miller told his visitors the stones measured four feet wide and weighed two thousand pounds.

"Is this the original mill?" Garrett had to know.

"No, that one started as a log building in the 1820s. This mill was built around 1869 when the old one burned." He dabbed his face with a bandanna handkerchief. "Tough times aren't restricted to the past. We deal with floods, and a tornado hit us in 2011—ripped off part of the roof. But with good insurance and the support of the community, we're grinding again."

"I guess tough people aren't restricted to the past," Garrett said as they headed for the mill's snack shop.

Approval shone from her eyes. "You've got that right. Fire, floods, and tornadoes have struck, all within the past few years. Still, Bridgeton refused to give up her bridge or her gristmill." She gestured toward the menu on the wall. "Fortunately, they haven't given up on locally made ice cream, either. How about persimmon—my favorite—or sweet potato pie?"

Garrett gulped. "Um, do they have strawberry? Lemon gelato?"

"Yes, but I'll bet you eat that all the time." Her full lip curled. "Don't you want to try something new on your vacation?"

It has to taste better than deep-fried candy bars. He'd never eaten a persimmon, so he opted for a sweet potato pie cone. Sitting with her at the last empty table on the mill's patio, he eyed it cautiously.

One bite hooked him. *Brown-sugar sweet. Mellow. Very rich.* "Sweet potatoes that have gone to heaven."

She licked her own cone with gusto. "I won't say I told you so."

He didn't know which seemed more delicious—the ice cream or the teasing smile she flung his way.

She held out her cone. "Want to try persimmon?"

He leaned toward her. "If you say it's good, I'm sure it is."

The challenge in her dark chocolate eyes melted into—what?

A warm shiver spiraled down his spine. He took a quick taste and sat back in the black metal chair. *Tangy-sweet...potent...*

She withdrew the cone, turned, and pointed. "The Case Cabin—the oldest in the county—is just down the street. Interested?"

"Sure." Good idea. If he sat here, looking at her, his ice cream might melt.

Thankfully, the weathered 1822 log cabin coaxed his mind back to Elijah Beal. Seba Case, who helped run the gift shop inside, pointed to the ax his ancestor, also named Seba, had used to build the one-room structure.

As Kendra perused cookbooks, baskets, and pottery, Garrett pictured his shivering forefather warming frozen hands and feet by the big stone fireplace, devouring hot corn pone and beans offered by hospitable hosts, reading his worn Bible by flickering candlelight, and praying for the people of Bridgeton who needed spiritual renewal.

"Garrett?"

Her voice startled him back to the twenty-first century.

Kendra stood near the cabin's open door, her head cocked. "Are you all right?" Her fine russet eyebrows crinkled together over her nose.

"I'm fine." He hastened out the door, onto the ramshackle front porch. "Just thinking about how it felt to wake up in this cabin every day."

"You acted as if someone hypnotized you. I don't think I've met a guy who's so into the past."

He longed to talk to her about his mission. "I've always liked history."

His high school history teacher would have rolled on the floor laughing.

"Maybe you'd like to see more of the downtown historic district?"

"Sure." He wondered what she thought of him. He didn't know what to think of him, either. God and Elijah Beal had turned his world upside down, and nothing could be the same again.

Kendra didn't expect Garrett to drool over the craft barns, booths, and shops as she did—and she was right. He did seem to enjoy the Bridgeton's other historical buildings: the 1878 house near the cabin, Crooks Manor, the Baldridge House, the Jones House, and the Masonic Lodge, all built during the 1800s and early 1900s. He also wanted to stop by the Methodist and Baptist churches. They weren't that old, built during the twentieth century. Their congregations, he said, had worshipped in log cabins back during the first half of the 1800s.

Why are you so interested in churches, Garrett?

She'd thought he would find local history trivial; good grief, the man lived in Washington, DC. The White House, the Declaration of Independence, and the Constitution occupied part of his everyday life. Why had he come to Parke County?

And will you come back?

There it was. The thought that wouldn't go away. She tried to squash it into submission, but the more she and Garrett wandered, the harder she found it to ignore those playful yet intense eyes that analyzed yet embraced the historic buildings, the amazing grin that transformed his precise features, the tall physique that made her feel feminine. *Finally, a man whose feet are bigger than mine!*

She needed to go home. Soon.

After they'd stuffed themselves with sati babi, she said, "It's been great, but I should prepare for classes tomorrow."

"Busy schedule?"

"I try to clear it during festival week, but yes, classes, homework to grade, and lots of flying with students." She concentrated on wiping sticky sauce from her fingers.

"I really appreciate your showing me around."

That warmth in his voice. She hated it. She loved it. "You're welcome." *I guess... .* She rose to toss her trash, mentally slapping herself upside the head as the dormant volcano inside her reawakened. *Have you forgotten his messing with Chase's life? Are you really going to trade your little brother's future for a pair of blue eyes and feet bigger than yours?*

The big feet followed Kendra through the growing twilight as she left their earlier leisurely pace behind. A mellow harvest moon peeked over the edge of the black horizon around Bridgeton.

Rats. The traitorous evening showed every intention of casting a romantic spell. She walked faster. He walked faster. When they reached their parking spot, she jumped into the Jeep, revving the engine even before Garrett reached the passenger side.

The moment he entered, the engine died.

Her Jeep never died!

She kicked the accelerator and tried again. Started. Died. Silence.

She didn't mean to look at him, but she did. The shadows couldn't hide the odd smile on his face, that glint in his eye. Desperately she hit the ignition again. This time the Jeep gave its usual vigorous roar. She threw it into reverse, flattening them against the seat, and wove past several slower cars, escaping onto the country roads she knew as well as she knew her driveway.

The welcome autumn wind cooled her hot cheeks and hardened her resolve. She yelled—"I'm taking a different route home"—and accelerated into the semidarkness.

"Fine." He sat stiff as a board, his eyes straight ahead. If

Garrett had entertained less-than-platonic notions, he'd probably lost them when she peeled out of the parking lot.

But just in case—*let's take a little ride you won't forget.*

Chapter 6

"Kendra, what did you do to Garrett?"

She jumped. Chase sounded exactly like their grandfather. She continued grading papers. "I don't know what you're talking about."

"Yes, you do." He pulled a chair to her desk and sat on it backwards. He lowered his chin, a junior version of Grandpa's flint-sharp gaze pressing on her.

"That's ridiculous." She applied her big-sister tone, though her heart sank as she remembered Garrett's terse good-bye when she dropped him off at the inn. "What makes you think I did something to Garrett?"

"I ran into him today on the town square. He seemed friendly enough, but when I mentioned your name, he looked as if he'd seen an orc from *The Lord of the Rings*." Chase glowered. "What did you do?"

Sometimes brothers caused more trouble than they were worth. "Excuse me. I didn't think I had to submit a report to you every time I go out."

Chase crossed his arms. "I don't hassle you about your boyfriends—"

"Oh really? What about the time you sprayed my prom date with the garden hose?"

Her change-the-subject tactic worked. He laughed. "Hey, I was only five years old. But you have to admit, the guy was a loser."

Eventually she'd realized the guy possessed the ambition of a garden slug.

Chase's grin faded. "I hate to bring this up, but I also saw Gregory for the scuzzball he was."

She winced. Her brother's immediate dislike for the guy had panned out more than he knew. Unknown to Chase—and to her, for two months—Gregory had been married. "Shall we discuss your girlfriends?"

"Okay, okay." He held up a hand. "Let's return to the real subject: Garrett. In getting acquainted with him, I'm making an important connection, one that may affect my future."

Don't I know it. She tried not to fidget. "I'm sorry if our not hitting it off has upset you."

" 'Not hitting it off'? I don't buy that." The grandpa gaze again. "The first time Garrett laid eyes on you at church, he looked as if he'd lost a hundred IQ points. You've tried to hide it, but you fell for him, too."

Please don't remind me. I'm doing this for you. "Nonsense." She stood. "We've only gone out once—"

"Twice, actually. My doing."

His smug smile ignited her ire. "You messed with my private life, Chase. Plus, you are making huge assumptions with no basis in fact."

He stood, too. "Don't play professor with me, Kendra. I know what I know. Why did you try to scare Garrett off?"

"How I relate to Garrett Beal is none of your business."

"Maybe not." He leaned across the desk, his face inches from hers. "But did you sabotage your friendship with him, hoping he'd back away from me?"

The kid always was too smart. Looking elsewhere would only confirm her brother's suspicions, so she gave him a withering glare she hoped would end the discussion.

"Aha!" Chase crowed as if he'd won a basketball bet, but fire sparked in his eyes. "Who's messing with whose life, Sis? I know you're trying to keep me here."

"What's wrong with Parke County?" The words burst from her. "Why do you want to leave home?"

"I just want to go where God leads me. Is that such a rotten thing?"

They were fighting about God. She couldn't believe this. "How can you be so sure God doesn't want you here?"

"I'm not sure. That's why I'm praying and exploring options. An internship with Garrett's company could be one of them. Maybe the best." He set his jaw. "I will pursue that possibility, Kendra. Whether you like it or not."

Hort always shared a grin with his elephant ear customers. Kendra, finished with classes and flying lessons, hoped her old friend could take his presupper break with her. *Tell me corny stories, Hort, even your elephant jokes, because I really could use a smile.*

Sure enough, he sat under his awning with a mug of hot cider and insisted on pouring one for her. His grin stretched even wider than usual.

"Life must be treating you well, Hort." *Better than me.*

"I'm doing good. Angie had another baby last month, a little boy, Carter Andrew."

"Congratulations, Hort!" Kendra knew how much he missed his daughter, who lived in Seattle.

"I have an unofficial grandbaby, too. You remember my niece, Lauren, who stayed with me awhile? She and Kyle had a little girl this past August, Lily Grace."

"The prettiest, sweetest baby girl in the world." The large older woman who brought them two smoking-hot elephant ears pulled from her pocket a photo of identical blond-haired boys hovering over a bright-eyed baby. "The twins think so, too."

"Right on all counts." Hort gestured toward the newcomer as Kendra exclaimed about the cute children. "This is Rose Hammond, their grandma. She and Al are helping me at the festival. I'm staying with them a couple of weeks in their RV at the Turkey Run Campground."

"I'm glad to meet you, Mrs. Hammond." Kendra shook hands then tackled the elephant ear.

Hort patted the picture and returned it to the smiling grandmother before she headed back to the stand. He shifted his chair toward Kendra. "Things are going great for me. How about you?"

"They're okay."

"Are they?"

Oh no, you don't, Hort. You might have talked me into spilling my guts when I was a kid, but no true confessions now. Kendra shrugged. "Not great, but no biggie. Life isn't perfect."

"Sure isn't. But it's good, because God is good."

"Yeah." *At least, this elephant ear is.*

"Chase came by. Seems worried about you."

"Worried?" She didn't mean to snap the word out like profanity.

"Concerned. He feels you don't want him to leave the area, yet senses God is directing him elsewhere."

Chase, you big mouth. She shifted in her chair, trying to untangle her thoughts and words. Finally she blurted, "I don't get this thing where God acts as a giant GPS who tells people where to go. Doesn't He give us brains to figure that out?"

"Yes, but He also wants us to look to Him before we set our plans in stone."

"But why would He want Chase to leave Indiana?" She couldn't keep the quaver out of her voice. "Chase could study for his master's at Rose-Hulman. He wouldn't have to leave home—"

"And leave you?"

Three quiet little words, but they pierced her as if she were a water balloon. Tears gushed down her face. She grabbed a paper napkin and tried to keep her sobs inside. "I helped raise him. He's all I have. You don't understand—"

"I don't?" A sad little smile stole onto his leathery face.

Kendra closed her eyes. Hort had lost his funny, loving wife, Kate, years before, and Angie had lived far away most of her adult life.

"Chase has to try his wings, Kendra." Hort took her hand. "You know how that feels, don't you? What if someone told you, you couldn't fly?"

Tears again, but she lifted her chin. "I'd like to see them try to stop me."

"So would I." His moist eyes twinkled.

She half chuckled, half moaned, "The older I grow, the less I like change."

Hort laughed outright. "You want to talk ancient? Just the other day, Noah and I went fishing together off the ark." He shook his head. "Kendra, you're far too much of an adventurer to give in to the moldy-oldie syndrome. Besides…"

"What?"

He leaned toward her like a conspirator. "God almost always keeps surprises up His sleeve."

Who is that guy?

Garrett, who had been mindlessly wandering Rockville's square, ducked into a craft tent. His frown deepened as he peered at the information shack.

A tall man with dark hair, graying at the temples, and shoulders like a gladiator's had stopped to talk to Kendra. A military guy, probably an officer. Garrett had seen dozens of them in Washington. The man spoke in a growling voice. Garrett couldn't detect what he was saying.

Kendra replied with her usual magnetic smile. She was shouldering her bag and leaving with this dude.

Garrett gritted his teeth. Had he somehow missed the minor information that she was dating G. I. Joe?

Chill, Beal. You hardly know her, and the last time you saw her, she drove you home like a NASCAR racer.

The man's hand touched the small of Kendra's back as they walked. Garrett wanted to punch him.

Amazing how a whole hour of Bible reading and prayer could go down the drain when someone crossed what he wanted. *Lord, I'm sorry—*

"Hey, Garrett. What's up?" Chase peered into the tent.

Garrett realized he'd ducked into a doggie-sweater booth. "I'm just between places." *What else can I say? "I'm spying on your sister"?*

"Oh." Chase gestured toward several food booths. "When you're finished, want to grab a snack?"

Garrett had decided to sever any connection with Kendra, nip his infatuation in the bud. Still, seeing her with that dude had made him feel as if he floated alone in an empty small-town sea. Chase, with his infectious laugh and incisive mind, offered a life preserver. "Sure."

"Have you ever eaten an elephant ear?"

"A what?"

"An elephant ear—big piece of hot fried bread with sugar and cinnamon on it. Trust me, once you've eaten one, you'll never live without them again." Chase sniffed the air like a hungry hound. "Let's go get 'em."

"Okay." Chase's giant intellect seemed superseded only by his enormous appetite.

"Besides, I want you to meet Hort."

"Hort?"

"Yeah, Horton Hayworth, the owner of Hort's Heavenly Elephant Ears."

Garrett blinked. Name had a Dr. Seuss sound to it. Nevertheless, he followed Chase, who threaded a path through the growing multitude.

He halted.

Kendra was crossing the street with her escort.

"Who's that guy?" Chase had spotted them.

Garrett almost grinned. *You sound like I did.*

"I don't know him." Chase headed for them, shoving Garrett in front. "Let's go say hi."

"Um—"

"Hey, Kendra!" Chase bellowed.

She turned and stared. So did a hundred other people, including her date.

Garrett pasted on a casual expression, following Chase as he hurried to his sister.

"Hi, I'm Kendra's brother." Chase, wearing an oversize smile, thrust a hand at the big guy. "This is our good friend Garrett Beal."

Ex-friend. Garrett saw it in Kendra's tight mouth.

But her gaze locked with his. His legs liquefied.

"Hello. I'm Roger Toggle." The man alternated glances between Kendra and Garrett.

"We were just heading for the food booths." Garrett tugged on Chase's elbow.

He didn't resist. "Yeah. You guys have fun at the festival. 'Bye."

Garrett strode away. Where did a first-class fool go to recover?

Walking beside him, Chase rolled his eyes. "I'll bet Mrs. Toggle pushed Kendra into a blind date." He snorted. "I should be glad Mrs. T. only bugs me about getting my hair cut."

Garrett wanted to change the subject. "Where's Hort's?"

Instant success. "Just down the street."

Soon they approached a stand with a white awning and a blue-and-white scrolled sign: Hort's Heavenly Elephant Ears. An elderly man was shoving golden platelike pastries through the order window to a large family.

"Hey, Hort. This is my friend Garrett, an engineer from Washington, DC. We're starving."

"Got an extra-big ear with your name on it." He cocked a fuzzy gray eyebrow at Garrett. "You want one?"

His stomach gave an unexpected growl. "Sounds like I'd better try one, too."

"Take a second to fry. I'll bring 'em out."

Sitting at a table under the awning, Garrett and Chase briefly switched to engineerese in a discussion about steel design. Spending substantial time with Chase appealed to him more and more. Garrett mentally began to dictate a high recommendation for Chase to his boss.

Hort plopped his delectable offerings on their table.

"Pull up a chair, Hort, if you have time." Chase patted the table.

"Always got time to meet a friend of yours. Plus, I need to take a load off more than I used to." Hort leaned back in the chair, his hands folded over a slight paunch under his apron. "Washington, huh? What brings you to Indiana?"

"Garrett taught a seminar at Rose-Hulman," Chase explained, "and now he's checking out the covered bridges."

"You've come to the right place. Which ones have you seen so far?"

"The bridges at Billie Creek and those in and near Bridgeton." Garrett stopped in the middle of a bite, trying not to remember Kendra at Bridgeton, issuing her ice cream cone challenge.

"Used to visit relatives in Bridgeton when I was a boy." Hort seemed to sense Garrett's unease. "Fished near the mill. Always went to VBS with my cousins. Always go to that church when I come to Parke County."

Wow. Sixty, maybe seventy years later, the old guy held fast to his faith and a church that had nurtured it.

"I did Bible school, too." Chase stopped eating long enough to contribute. "Now I help with the kids at our church whenever I can."

Unexpected longing welled up in Garrett. He'd enjoyed a

model suburban childhood, but talking to Chase and Hort, his life felt like he'd been building using only half a blueprint.

"I'll come to your church Sunday, Chase." Garrett had considered going elsewhere, but saying it aloud firmed his resolve.

He told Hort, "I visited the Bridgeton church building— "

"Wonderful people there. God has scattered His wonderful people all over Parke County, in all kinds of churches." Wise brown eyes probed Garrett's. "I'm sure He's done the same in Washington, DC."

"I'm sure He has, too." Garrett's parents clammed up when he talked about his faith, but Chase and Hort seemed to welcome spiritual subjects. Garrett ventured, "I only became a Christian this past January. I've attended several churches, but I haven't found one yet where I feel comfortable."

"How did you get acquainted with Jesus Christ?" Chase leaned forward.

"It's a long story—"

"I always have time to hear something like this." Hort gave an emphatic nod.

Encouraged, Garrett continued, "My ninety-five-year-old great-grandfather passed away recently." He focused on rubbing a black speck from the table. "Before he died, he told me he'd made a big mistake in abandoning his childhood faith. He gave me a journal, written back in the 1830s by his great-great-great-grandfather, Elijah Beal, a circuit rider in southwestern Indiana." Remembering his faded, loving face, Garrett bowed his head. "Great-grandpa made me promise I'd read it."

Hort's knotty old hand pressed his shoulder. Garrett raised his eyes to see Chase's widen.

"I only read it because he asked me," Garrett continued. "But the more I read, the more I wanted to be like Elijah. He was an adventurer, braving the wilderness to preach to people and help them." Garrett shrugged. "I lived in a 'me' cocoon: work, money, entertainment. The more I read Elijah's writings, the more I wanted to know the God he knew. I read the Bible and decided to follow Jesus."

Chase abandoned his elephant ear. "So you came to Parke County—"

"Because I sensed it was the next step in my spiritual pilgrimage." Garrett nodded. "Someday I want to visit the Holy Land and follow Jesus' footsteps. Checking out Elijah's territory is a start."

"Awesome!" Chase knocked knuckles with Garrett.

"You're on a journey of faith." Hort's face shone. "Abraham, Isaac, Jacob, and Joseph took those, too—though Joseph didn't have much of a choice." He chuckled. "Ended up in jail."

"Hopefully, God hasn't included that in my itinerary."

"You could always stay in the Jail House Inn down on the square so you'll be prepared," Chase kidded. "Original drunk tank from the 1800s, iron bars, the works."

"I saw that. Looks great, but the teddy bears would miss me."

"Oh no." Chase rolled his eyes. "You aren't—"

"Oh yes, I am. Thanks to my secretary's reserving the last available room in Parke County, I share a bridal suite with a gazillion teddy bears."

Later, as Garrett, stuffed with elephant ears, lay awake in the heart-shaped bed, he couldn't recall an evening with friends that matched the one he'd just spent, with alternating friendly gibes, engineering talk, and rich spiritual discussion. Hort, the Dr. Seuss guy, knew more about the Bible than Garrett anticipated learning in a lifetime. He also was mining valuable tidbits of theology and Christian living from Kendra's kid brother... .

He wished she would forget that other guy and go out with him again.

What would it be like to share his spiritual life with an intelligent, beautiful woman like her?

Chapter 7

"Please, Kendra!" Chase blocked her exit to the cabin's deck.

"Chase, what part of *no* don't you understand?"

"But this guy's worked hard to learn the books of the Bible. I told him you would take him on an airplane ride this week. I *promised*, Kendra."

She considered throwing her briefcase at her brother. "You had no business promising something that involved me. I worked at the festival all weekend. I'm behind in planning lessons and grading exams—"

Huge puppy eyes. "But Hort and I have been working with him during the festival."

"During the festival?" She stared.

"Yeah, he'd show up at Hort's stand, and one of us would talk with him about the Bible. His parents don't know the Lord—"

"Chase, stop." Her forehead pounded as if the ISU band were marching across it. She slammed a mug of water into the microwave and faced him. "Do not speak to me for fifteen minutes. Then perhaps we can discuss this without bloodshed. Do I make myself clear?"

He nodded and left.

She stomped onto the deck with her tea, and sat, inhaling the forest's musky fragrance. Someday, when money wasn't tight, she'd buy a cushy chaise lounge where she could lie in a fetal position on days like this.

Later she'd call Sarah and share her woes. Right now, she needed quiet.

The sunset's brilliant ribbons of color began to calm her angst.

If only I could stay here forever, God.

Chase couldn't have picked a worse time to hit her up for "free" airplane rides. She absorbed the fuel and other costs, something he conveniently forgot. Her Jeep's mechanic, during a routine maintenance check, found problems with its ignition and brakes that cost her a bundle, chomping a bite out of her Ladyhawk fund.

On top of everything, she'd had to rescue her last flight student, herself, and northern Terre Haute from his mistakes.

Her cell vibrated. She checked it. Roger. Nice guy, but did she want to see him again? If she hadn't met Garrett…*ack!* She'd crossed Garrett off her list, right? He'd no doubt crossed her off after their wild night ride back from Bridgeton.

Men. Why waste these precious moments of solitude fuming about them?

Kendra fixed her eyes on one gilded, rose-colored cloud.

"Be still, and know that I am God." She'd memorized very little scripture, but that one from the Psalms had stuck in her heart. She let her shoulders droop, her head fall back.

"Be still." God always helped her manage her heavy teaching load.

"Be still." She forgave her lousy students and tried to remember the joy of flying with the good ones.

Chase's pleading face rose in her mind, along with those of little mentees he'd foisted on her before, boys he'd taught the

Gospel. As she flew them through the heavens, they marveled at the Creator they'd come to know.

She couldn't turn this kid down, though she felt like throwing her brother out of the cockpit.

"Be still." Kendra uncurled clenched fingers.

She'd never figure out guys. Never. How could she manage the recurring storm of painful Chase emotions that pingponged inside her like hailstones?

"What if someone told you, you couldn't fly?" Hort's words flitted at her mind, persistent sparrows at a window.

Why did Garrett affect her so strongly?

Yet Roger did not, even though he'd been fun and attentive during their second date.

"Be still, and know that I am God."

You're God, and I'm not, right? She sighed and watched several sky-ribbons swirl into soft lavender twilight.

Taking one more sip, Kendra checked her phone's clock. Time to talk to Chase. She'd call Roger later. And Garrett? She rolled her eyes heavenward.

You made these men, Lord. I'm glad You understand them.

Garrett didn't consider himself an egotist, but most women who looked at him seemed to like what they saw.

This one didn't. Kendra, turning from checking her plane's landing gear, met him with eyes that first widened, then blazed like rocket boosters.

"Behold my Bible student." Chase bowed to Garrett with a flourish. "He can pronounce the Old Testament prophets and even spell them."

Oookay. Garrett had no idea why Chase proclaimed this like a herald, but hopefully his tactic—whatever it was—would calm Kendra. He'd only let Chase talk him into another plane ride because she'd invited him. He'd hoped the summons presented the beginnings of a renewal of their friendship.

Obviously, she regretted the effort. Surprisingly, she glared at Chase more than him.

"I haven't flown with you in ages, Red Wonder." Hort, yelling over the plane's engine noise, hugged Kendra. "Nice of you to take us up today."

Some of her rigidity melted. She didn't roll out the red carpet as she opened the cockpit's passenger door, but she said hello to everyone, including Garrett.

Hort, when you've finished helping me with the Bible, would you teach me about women?

Hort climbed into the back seat. Chase wedged in beside him, leaving Garrett no choice but to sit in front where Kendra could glower at him the entire flight.

He wondered what minute remark would set her off. *Why are you so flammable, Kendra?*

He tried to think positive, however, as she taxied down the runway. Flying this little plane kept her occupied.

It kept him praying.

Garrett tried not to clutch the armrest as they took off. They soared higher. His stomach sank lower. He dared not look at Kendra. He briefly tried to appreciate fluffy banks of clouds so close he felt he could open the window and grab handfuls… of nothing… . He closed his eyes and sank back into the seat.

Chase's voice floated across his shoulder. "Betcha you can't say the books of the Old Testament, Garrett."

"Bet I can." Spouting tricky names while riding in this glorified windup toy four thousand feet above the ground made no sense. Hey, why not? Better to die with those words on his lips than others. He took a deep breath. "Genesis. Exodus—"

"Leviticus." Chase.

"Numbers." Hort joined in the roll call. "Deuteronomy."

Good. Garrett always struggled with that incomprehensible mouthful. "Joshua."

"Judges." Chase.

"Ruth." Hort.

The rhythm of reciting the ancient names calmed his stomach, his mind. His heart rate? Not so much. But he chalked that up to Kendra's nearness.

Dark-lashed brown eyes scanned the instruments, the sky, the clouds. He could have studied all day—covertly, of course—the curve of her creamy cheek and ripe lips, slightly open as she adjusted the controls.

"You're blowing it, Beal." Chase's voice interrupted his pleasant musings. "What comes after Proverbs?"

He scoured his foggy mind. "Um…um…"

"Ecclesiastes." A tiny smile sneaked across Kendra's mouth. She threw him a glance that made him feel like he could fly without the plane.

If Kendra hated him, why did she look at him that way?

Overcompensating, he almost yelled, "Song of Solomon!"

"Amos. Obadiah." Joining in again, she grinned and sent him another zinger glance.

"Jonah," he retorted. *Enough, Kendra. No more killing me and then kissing me with your eyes. I'm going to find out what you're really thinking, if it's the last thing I do.*

But he'd wait until they landed.

Otherwise, it may be *the last thing.*

Chase, you scheming scuzzball. How could he lie in order to get her and Garrett together?

She'd deal with Chase later.

Although she had to give him credit. He'd calmed Garrett with a tactic he'd used with kids she'd taken on flights: saying the books of the Bible. Big eyed as he recited biblical names, Garrett seemed even cuter than those previous young passengers.

The man appeared so innocent, not like a brother-napper. He looked way, way too good. How could she stay mad at him if he kept this up?

She hated to scare Garrett again, but she had to kill off this relationship once and for all.

"Galatians." Unaware of her plan, Chase continued the game.

"Ephesians," Hort said.

"Philippians. Colossians." She began to ease the control wheel back, pulling into a smooth, steep climb.

Garrett started to chime in as before, then flattened against the seat as the plane rose, turned belly up, and zoomed down in a large loop.

"First Thessalon–i–*aaaaaaaaaaaaaaaaans!*"

Perhaps it was just as well the roller-coaster flight kept him speechless—sans oxygen, actually—until Kendra touched down. Theoretically, his entire body should have turned to jelly.

Instead, resolve, like a hard spare skeleton, supported him so he could unbuckle his seat belt, swing his cockpit door open, and disembark.

Chase, who also looked a little dazed, crawled out the back. Garrett saw Kendra's profile as she helped Hort out on her side.

"Are you all right?" Garrett marveled that the old guy could walk.

"I'm great. Used to ride in my friend's crop duster until a few years ago."

While relief filled Garrett that the man hadn't died of a heart attack, he wished Hort looked a little pale, a bit weak-kneed. Then Garrett could really blast Kendra into the stratosphere.

He started to walk to the hangar but stopped. Kendra already had turned back to the plane, probably making her escape to Chicago or New York or Timbuktu. Well, she wasn't going to get away with it.

"Kendra." He strode back to the pilot's side of the cockpit, slipped in front of its door, and crossed his arms. "I want to talk to you."

Could ice burst into flame? Fire shot from Garrett's glacier eyes, igniting her own and sending hot-cold tremors down her body. "Excuse me. I have to secure the plane."

"Fine. I'll follow you around, I'll sit outside your classroom, I'll even go up in that thing again, if I have to." Unblinking, he moved closer, lowering his head until she could practically count his eyelashes. "But we need to talk."

"I don't think so." She gulped at his nearness and then stabbed her hips with her hands.

"Hey, some of this is my fault." Chase shook her shoulder. "Though it's your problem, too, Kendra."

"*My* problem?" She whirled around and glared at him. "What—"

"I think," Hort said, "that we should pray together."

She and the guys froze at the elephant ear maker's quiet but firm voice.

"Here?" She stared. "Now?"

"Here and now. I'll keep it brief." Hort grasped her hand. "All join hands and hearts with me, please, as we talk to God."

His words made her realize what she'd forgotten—God was watching this whole scenario. So she took Chase's hand, though she felt like smacking him. Thank heaven, she didn't have to touch Garrett.

He probably felt the same way. Glowering, he grasped Chase's and Hort's hands.

Hort kept his prayer brief and to the point. "Father, thank You that You love us all the time. Thank You for these special children of Yours. But right now, they're fighting, and they need Your help to straighten this out. Please help them do it. Amen."

He dropped her hand. Kendra had barely opened her eyes when he turned to go. Over his shoulder, Hort said, "I'm headed back to my stand. You all work this out like adults, and I'll be praying for you. If you need my help, you know where to find me."

They stared at each other in silence.

"Well…" Chase fidgeted. "I guess we'd better talk. I don't have a class until two, and you don't have any this morning, Kendra."

He knew her schedule too well. "I still have to secure the plane and go through the checklist."

"Go ahead. We'll wait. Won't we, Garrett?"

Long pause. Then a look that turned her cold, yet made her sizzle. "I'll wait."

Chapter 8

Kendra had tried to veto the plan for this discussion to take place on her deck. Her deck equaled her space, her oasis where she relaxed into who she really was.

"Where else?" Chase argued. "It's a nice day, and we gotta talk someplace where we can yell."

In a way, she wished Garrett would yell. He sat across from her, as far away as he could without falling off the deck, drinking cider with robotic movements.

Chase sat on a built-in bench near Kendra. "I have to leave soon, so I'll apologize first." He turned to Garrett. "I'm sorry I lied to you. Kendra did not invite you to fly with us."

His mouth fell open. "Wha—"

"I'll explain in a second. I need to apologize to Kendra, too."

"I'm all ears." She crossed her arms.

"I was wrong. I let you believe I had invited a kid to take an airplane ride with us as a reward for learning about the Bible. I didn't exactly lie—"

"You didn't?" Her cheeks heated again.

"Everything I told you was true. Garrett did visit Hort's to learn more about the Bible. We helped him. He doesn't come from a Christian background." Chase was doing the puppy-dog-eye thing again.

"You just didn't happen to mention our Bible-studying passenger was at least twenty years older than usual." Kendra rolled her eyes heavenward.

"You hatched a pretty elaborate scheme involving both of us." Garrett broke in. Kendra could imagine his as the cool voice in the midst of a corporate boardroom controversy. "May I ask why you went to all the trouble?"

No more games, Chase. Be honest.

"Several reasons. Good ones." The cute-puppy look vanished. "Garrett, I think you're a great guy."

"Right." Garrett maintained the expressionless look and tone. Still, Kendra sensed his hurt at her brother's deception.

"Seriously." Chase faced him. "Your faith, your intellect, and your knowledge of your field amaze me. I also think you like my sister. A lot. And she likes you."

Not that honest. Kendra wanted to stuff a sock into his mouth.

"You could have fooled me." Garrett glared at her. "You've tried twice to kill me—"

She leaped to her feet. "Don't be ridiculous."

"Ridiculous?" He jumped up, too.

She snorted. "A little Jeep ride and a couple of loops in the air don't constitute attempted murder—"

"You nearly gave me a heart attack. You've aged me fifty years in ten days—"

"Should I ring a bell?" Chase jumped between them like a referee. "At least, let's conclude round one. Okay?"

Kendra hated the taint of their discord echoing through the peaceful forest. She sat.

Garrett returned to his corner.

"May I finish?" Chase dropped onto the bench. His tone returned to a normal level. "Bottom line, I think you would be great together, but you two can discuss that after I leave for class."

"We probably will." Garrett's eyes bored into him. "But did you think a relationship between us would solidify an internship for you at my company?"

"How dare you?" Kendra stood again. She wanted to pop that stiff, controlled face in the chops. "How dare you insinuate such a thing?"

"Chill, Kendra. It's a reasonable question." Chase returned Garrett's steely gaze. "The possibility crossed my mind. But I decided to pursue a friendship with you, regardless." He walked to Garrett and extended his hand. "I still want to be your friend, if you'll forgive me."

Despite her annoyance, she couldn't help feeling proud of him. But wouldn't reconciliation between them increase Chase's chances of going to DC?

Garrett, reaching to shake Chase's hand, paused. "Kendra, do you want me to stay friends with Chase?"

"Uh—"

"No, she doesn't." No puppy-dog look on Chase's face now.

Garrett's hand dropped. So did his controlled mask. "What's with you, Kendra?"

"She doesn't want me to leave Parke County." Chase's mahogany eyes glowed like embers.

Kendra moved to a different corner of the deck. Clasping herself with taut arms, she turned away. The woods blurred into a messy landscape.

Footsteps from Garrett's corner. His magnetic presence loomed behind her. "So you think I'm taking your brother away from you."

"We were doing fine, just the two of us, before you came." The stupid words spurted from her before she could stop them.

"Remember, we're being honest?" Chase's voice. "You've known for ages I didn't intend to stay at Rose-Hulman."

Her traitor mind played back images of Chase filling out

applications, collecting references, making phone calls the past year. *Of course, you're right.*

Her mouth refused to admit it.

Garrett's voice again. "Kendra, do you want me to leave?"

Garrett's lungs felt as if they were made of concrete.

Silence.

She shook her head in a slow right-left, right-left no.

A silent *"Yesss!"* coursed through Garrett.

Chase blew his nose, which sounded like a semitrailer's air horn. He said, "So you won't fight my friendship with Garrett, no matter what?"

The head shake again. "You tried to tell me how you felt. I didn't want to believe you."

Garrett's hand met Chase's as if they'd cued each other.

"Thanks, Kendra." Though Garrett exulted at her affirmation, he didn't know what else to say.

"Yeah, thanks, Sis." Chase patted her shoulder. He checked the time on his phone. "Man, I'd better take off for class—"

"Not so fast." His sister wheeled around. "I don't remember granting you forgiveness for being such a pain."

Now Chase crossed his arms. "I haven't heard you apologize for messing with my life, either."

For a moment, Garrett thought the two fiery redheads would explode into a blowup scene of movie proportions.

Finally Kendra shrugged with a get-it-over-with gesture. "All right. Chase, I'm sorry. I still don't understand why you want to leave...but I'll try."

He hugged her. "Apology accepted. I'm sorry I tried to throw you and Garrett together." For the first time that day, his eyes gleamed with mischief. "Though I don't think you really suffered—"

"Okay, okay. I forgive you." She flapped an arm at him. "Get out of here."

"I thought you wanted me to stay around forever—"

"*Leave*, already."

Throwing a huge grin over his shoulder, Chase dashed inside the house.

Standing beside Kendra, Garrett heard the cough of her brother's car and crunch of gravel as he left the driveway.

She'd better do this before she backed out. Biting her lip, Kendra said, "I'm sorry I freaked you with the Jeep and plane rides."

Slowly he turned those cobalt eyes on her. "Now that I understand more about you and Chase, I can see why you'd do that. Sort of." He shook his head. "I guess I didn't get why you liked me one moment and—"

"Tied you to Ladyhawk's tail the next?"

He gave a cautious chuckle.

I'm kidding, okay? "I really do apologize. I forget not everybody feels as comfortable as I do in a plane."

"I don't drag race through forests at night, either," Garrett said with a half smile.

"You must lead a very boring life."

His eyes frosted over again. He sat and sipped his cider.

Too late to stuff a sock in her mouth. She dropped into her camp chair. *Oh Lord, what do I do now? He'll leave and never come back.*

"Perhaps it is boring. I used to think my life was normal."

Was Garrett still speaking to her? He appeared to be talking to his cider mug. "But coming here has changed my outlook. Who says my life should be 'normal'? Not God."

At least he'd included her in sorting out his thoughts, though he'd lapsed into silence again.

She shared the quiet, now glad they'd talked on her deck. Summoning her courage and the best smile she could muster, Kendra said, "Maybe you could delete my last remark? In fact, could we delete everything that's happened the past few days and start over?"

The look he gave her pulled her to her feet again. She

crossed to the bench, sat beside him, and held out her hand. "Hi. My name is Kendra Atkinson."

For the first time that day, a sunrise smile spread from his mouth to his eyes. He grasped her hand. "Hi. I'm Garrett Beal, and the pleasure is definitely mine."

Chapter 9

Garrett had told Kendra he trusted her to behave this afternoon.

Now watching from the Jeep's passenger's side, he saw her jump behind the wheel again, that adventurous glint in her eye. Next time he'd offer to drive.

Kendra slammed the door. "Ready to visit some bridges?"

He gave her a thumbs-up.

She peeled out. Did she know no other way to exit a driveway? Still, he found the bumpy, weaving ride through the brilliant fall woods and farmland exhilarating. Was it because she rode the vehicle like a half-wild horse?

Gravel roads didn't bother her in the least. He found it refreshing that she didn't fuss about dust in her hair, which she wore in a french braid today. He liked it better lying thick and wavy down her back. This way, though, he only fought a third-grade urge to give it a yank, rather than run his fingers through it.

She seemed more relaxed after their talk two days before,

as if she'd settled things about Chase, about him. *Thank you, Hort. And thank You, Lord.*

Kendra slowed briefly when, rounding a bend, they encountered dozens upon dozens of pumpkins. He'd seen them piled in front of discount stores and at the festival. They looked almost unnatural scattered in a field.

He glanced at Kendra. She had to have seen this scene a hundred times, yet she looked as if God had thrown her a surprise party.

"Aren't the pumpkins awesome? I *love* fall."

She personified autumn, her hair outshining the glory of the leaves. Her russet sweater accented her peach-colored cheeks and lips. He almost forgot about their covered bridge tour until the Zach Cox Bridge loomed before them, the second shortest in Parke County, only fifty-something feet long. Kendra parked, and he jumped out, scanning the bridge's entrance. "Britton portal," he told her. "More squared-off entrance than the Daniels bridges that have curved entrances. Those two guys built most of the bridges in Parke County, I guess."

The Harry Evans Bridge, which they visited next, also had been built by Britton about the same time, 1908. After Garrett had checked out the bridge's construction, they wandered down the country road awhile.

"Lots of old coal mines in the hills around here," Kendra said, "and a really deep air shaft. Seems like every year, some kids or out-of-town visitors decide to explore them. Not a good idea."

"I'll resist the urge. Your driving is adventure enough for me."

She eyed him reproachfully, a smile teasing the corners of her mouth. "I thought I'd behaved quite well."

"The day isn't over yet." He grinned, but she wasn't the one that concerned him. *I hope I can behave, too—no unreal expectations, no demands, just time together.*

With an effort, he made himself focus on the next covered bridge. As she pulled over, he started as he took in the size of the thing. It had to measure at least two hundred fifty feet long across rippling Big Raccoon Creek. "Whoa, another Burr arch two-span." He read the inscription over the entrance: "Roseville Bridge. Hey, Info Lady, I thought we were going to Rosedale."

"Both towns were only a few miles apart, named after the same settler. Rosedale happens to be the one that survived."

As always, he enjoyed checking out its frame and making notes.

She pointed to the western entrance. "Doc Wheat lived near here, an herbalist who charged a dollar for treatments, no matter what. People traveled from as far as Chicago to be treated by Doc Wheat. A real character. He didn't trust banks and hid all his money in jars on his property, so people dug around there for years afterward."

"Surely this place wouldn't generate characters," Garrett raised an eyebrow.

"I have no idea what you're talking about," she said loftily.

Kendra clumped the oak boards of the bridge's floor like a child, and he joined in. They clogged to the end of the long, wooden tunnel, laughing. He'd always enjoyed studying bridges, but she made it a celebration.

"Are we headed to Rosedale now?" he asked as they walked back to the Jeep.

"We won't find any other bridges there, but yes, we'll drive through the town on the way to the Thorpe Ford Covered Bridge." She looked at him curiously.

Was he ready to share his true quest? His family thought he was nuts, but Chase and Hort reacted positively. Would Kendra? Garrett said, "My ancestor, Elijah Beal, preached in several towns in this part of Indiana during the 1830s, including Rosedale. He was a circuit rider."

"Awesome." Her smile encouraged him. "How did you find that out?"

"I inherited his journal from my grandfather right before he passed away. In reading it, I learned Elijah rode throughout this area. Business brought me here, but the covered bridge study grant and checking out Elijah's movements are keeping me in Indiana the next couple of weeks."

He thought of that first Sunday at Kendra's church, when he'd spotted her praying in a front pew. "I visited your church in the first place because Elijah preached to that congregation during the 1830s, when they were meeting in the log courthouse."

Kendra's eyes widened. "My grandma's family has attended there more than a hundred years, but I didn't know our church went back that far."

They'd reached the Jeep. On impulse, he opened the driver's door for her and gestured like a doorman.

She grinned. "You're certainly full of surprises, today, Mr. Engineer."

"Me?" Sitting in the Jeep with a backdrop of sunset splendor behind her, she outshone any expectations he'd had of Indiana. He couldn't help taking her hand and looking into those rich, earth-brown eyes. "Professor, you define the word."

Chapter 10

An outdoorsman, he wasn't. But Hort had issued an invitation Garrett couldn't refuse.

"You two and Chase come camp with us at Turkey Run. Nice and quiet since the festival ended, and the trees are at peak color."

Garrett and Kendra had run into Hort in Rockville as they pushed bikes down Ohio Street.

Kendra acted as if Hort handed them front row tickets to the NBA finals. She turned to Garrett. "I own camping gear. Maybe we could camp there the weekend before you leave?"

Faced with her joyous response, how could he say no?

"Um, sure." At least, Indiana's open fields and forests didn't seem so foreign now. "You think Chase will come, too?"

"If we feed him, he will come—and camping food is the best." Grinning, she turned back to Hort. "I'll call you to finalize things."

"Sounds good." He squinted an eye at Garrett. "You coming over tomorrow night?"

"Sure." Garrett genuinely looked forward to another Bible lesson with Hort.

Hort eyed their bikes. "Looks like you're gonna get your exercise. More bridges?"

Garrett nodded. "Headed to Montezuma. Several out that way."

Hort winked at Kendra and chuckled. "You told him what people around here used to call them, didn't you?"

She shook her head, a peachy flush rising on her cheeks. "We'd better go. Talk to you later, Hort."

They waved good-bye and rode to the north edge of Rockville. He marveled at the now-quiet roads. Cruising past red barns and farmhouses with laundry dancing on clotheslines, he felt as if he'd cycled into an earlier century, especially when they encountered horse-drawn buggies. He'd heard a large Amish population lived in Parke County. Bearded fathers and bonneted mothers drove along the road, little heads bobbing behind them.

He glanced back occasionally, making sure he wasn't outpacing Kendra. Garrett often biked to work because no sane person in DC drove unless he had to. On weekends he occasionally cycled twenty-five miles, the approximate distance of their route today.

"Bridge ahead," he called, in case he was blocking her view. They pulled up to Melcher Bridge, another built by J. Daniels. No signature arched entrance, though. Someone must have changed that to the flat portal. Garrett parked the bike and drank from his water bottle. He and Kendra walked to a golden poplar and plopped down to watch Leatherwood Creek flow under the bridge.

"Used to be a railway station near here," Kendra said. "You'd never know it now, would you?"

"Couldn't be much quieter." He leaned against the tree and closed his eyes. "Think I'll take a little late-afternoon nap."

She poked him with a stick. "You're going to collapse on me this early in the ride?"

He grabbed the stick and tossed it into the creek. "You noticed I stayed ahead of you?"

"We'll see how long that lasts."

He enjoyed a few sparks in her eyes, as long as they didn't burst into flame. But he liked them gentle, too. "I've found the bridges very interesting—though I wouldn't have enjoyed them half as much without you."

Her eyes did soften, but she looked down, scooping up colorful leaves, absentmindedly arranging them in a bouquet. "Do you really find bridges fascinating?"

"Yes, of all my projects, I like them best."

She didn't scratch her head, but she looked as if she wanted to. "You must feel about them the way I do about flying and my plane. I want to be Ladyhawk's sole owner."

She hadn't said that before. "How many owners are there?"

"Only two, Terry MacPherson and I." Her face brightened. "Now Terry has offered me a great price on his share. I don't know if or when I can do it, but I'll knock on every door I can."

She sounded absolutely hungry. *Does the plane mean that much to her?* A twinge of jealousy tugged at him. *So she's passionate about it. She's passionate about everything. You like her that way.*

"Well, guess we should check out the bridge." He rose and dragged her, laughing, to her feet.

He didn't release her right hand.

She glanced down, then up, and smiled.

When they reached Melcher Bridge, he made himself drop her hand—for a while—so he could take notes. The bridge was another one-span built in 1896, the abutments constructed of shale and limestone. Someone had reinforced them later with poured concrete. Wooden shingles covered the roof. He finished and said, "Want to walk through it with me?"

Their walk-through had become a ritual—though he didn't regard it as routine. How could he, with her leggy stride matching his steps, eyes shining in the shadows, and now her warm fingers intertwined with his?

They'd walked halfway across when he said, "What was that Hort mentioned? A nickname for these bridges?"

Even in the dimness, he could see her face change color. "Hort can be ornery at times."

"So what did they call them?"

She hesitated then shrugged. "Kissing bridges."

Hort, you just had to bring up the subject. Kendra loosened her hand from Garrett's.

"Why did they call them that, Kendra?" His small smile shot her heart rate up to the rafters.

"It shouldn't take an engineer to figure that out." She tried to assume the same tone she'd used sharing other bridge facts. "Courting couples a century ago didn't have much privacy. They often took carriage rides through as many bridges as they could."

"Smart people, right?"

She didn't dare look at him. *Try to keep things light.* Garrett would leave soon, and she'd be lucky if he sent her a Christmas card.

Roger, on the other hand, had told her he'd be stationed at Grissom Reserve Air Base, little more than a hundred miles away.

She walked faster toward the bridge's end.

Garrett's long legs kept him right beside her.

The end at last! Kendra stretched, almost as if reaching a finish line.

"Why the rush? Isn't cycling enough cardio for you?"

His grin annoyed her—and stole what breath she had left.

"Are we going to race back to the bikes, too?"

Duh. She hadn't thought about having to walk through the bridge again.

He said, "I'm warning you, I'll win this time."

She tried to quell the shiver of alarm and delight at his words. *Grow up, Kendra.*

She gave Garrett a cool smile and lifted her chin. "I think I'll take it a little slower. We still have a long ride this afternoon."

The thought of several more hours together warmed, and scared, her again, but she turned and began her stroll.

He didn't take her hand. He stayed a short distance behind, checking more bridge details.

So much for getting too serious. First he acted as if he would kiss her. Now he ignored her. What was she supposed to think?

Halfway back, though, she realized he was following at about the right speed so he could watch her walk.

Not knowing what else to do, she continued, eyes straight ahead.

I'll gain the upper hand at the next bridge. Somehow. Some way.

Garrett wondered if Kendra would mind a side trip. "I want to visit Oakland Cemetery here in Montezuma."

"A cemetery?"

He paused. "Elijah's buried there."

She'd mentioned a visit to the Wabash River shoreline, but now she surprised him with, "Let's go to the cemetery first." He gave her a grateful smile. They biked through town, stopping at an ornate black iron gate arched over a grassy road.

Garrett pulled a Google map from his bike pack. "According to this, we should find his grave there." He pointed to a section where early settlers were interred.

They parked their bikes nearby. Garrett searched among weathered grave markers, some leaning with age. There it was. He stopped in front of the simple white tablet and read aloud, "Elijah Beal, born December 21, 1811. Died November 28, 1869. Aged fifty-seven years, eleven months, and seven days." He knelt and rubbed his fingers on the lettering under the dates. "Then said I, here am I; send me. Isaiah 6:8."

Kendra knelt beside him as the Indian summer breeze played a rustling hymn on dry leaves.

"Elijah preached wherever he could. He went hungry, especially when people disliked his messages about sin. Sometimes they threatened him and ran him out of town." He shook his head. "I'm not the hero Elijah was."

She covered his hand with hers. "None of us are heroes like him."

Comforted, he bowed his head and whispered, "Lord, help me to know You the way Elijah did."

Garrett still felt unworthy of such a thing, yet he had to ask. *Lord, please be with me as You were with Elijah. Help me follow You.*

He tried to clear his mind and listen. No great thoughts came, only the sense that God had listened to him, too.

He looked up and squeezed Kendra's hand. "Here's his wife's tombstone." He read the faded letters: "Mary Ann, wife of Elijah."

Kendra touched the marker gently then rose with him to walk back to the bikes.

Not every woman would understand his need to stop here. He slipped his arm around Kendra. "Thanks for coming with me."

As they retrieved their bikes, he asked, "You want to lead the way to the Wabash?"

They backtracked and headed to the forested shoreline, where they sat on a bank and watched the green and gold waters glide past. Garrett said, "Much bigger than I expected, and certainly more beautiful. Hard to believe this is the same river Elijah describes. Every mention he makes involves a flood or drowning."

"The Wabash can be dangerous, but I've always sort of regarded it as a friend." She knelt and swished her hand in the water. She looked up at him. "So Elijah settled here in Montezuma?"

"Yes. He rode the circuit for years and eventually married the daughter of one of the settlers he'd visited—"

"*She* probably fed him well." Kendra's smile helped him lighten up.

"He mentions that Mary Ann was a good cook." He grinned. "Judging from the engraving in the front of the book, Elijah needed someone to put a few pounds on him. Looked like a long-haired scarecrow."

"Did he still ride the circuit after he married?"

"Yes, unlike most riders, he carried on awhile before he settled in Montezuma. Elijah's superiors did not want him to marry, but he finally talked them into seeing his viewpoint."

Kendra's eyes sparked. "I'm not sure I care much for these 'superiors.'"

"They weren't trying to be mean. They knew the rider's family would suffer long absences. An income often paid in cents rather than dollars, shoe leather, a few yards of cloth here, a pouch of corn there." Garrett shook his head. "Dangerous lifestyle, too."

"Mary Ann must have been one strong woman."

"True. I'm glad they had each other. I can't imagine trying to live that kind of life alone." He turned his gaze from the river to Kendra, watching her cheeks pink.

He smiled. "I hate to leave Elijah's town, but, with three more bridges to see, we'd better go."

Perhaps Garrett still felt prayerful. In that case, Kendra's scheme wouldn't be necessary. As they approached Sim Smith Bridge, however, she pondered the inevitable truth that these kissing bridges could cast their spell on a man.

Garrett pulled out his phone and began his study-the-bridge routine.

Kendra followed, lowering her voice. "You sure you want to walk through? Maybe we could just bike across—fast."

He looked at her as if she'd lost her mind. "Why? I want to study it."

"Reports that this bridge is haunted have been circulating since 1900—"

"Oh brother." He rolled his eyes. "Who or what haunts Sim Smith? Bogeymen? Should I look for vampires hanging from the rafters and include them in my reports?"

"No vampires, but—"

"But what?"

"At each entrance, people have reported hearing a horse and buggy approaching the other side. But none ever appears. And—"

"There's more?"

"Two teens reported that a gigantic Native American woman carrying a papoose appeared."

"Seriously?" He shook his head.

"Seriously. Check the Covered Bridge Festival website if you don't believe me."

"All right, I'll go along with this absurdity." He threw his arms open wide and yelled, "How tall was she?"

"Around eight feet—"

"I've heard stupid urban myths, but this one beats them all." He headed for the bridge then turned, eyes glinting with annoyance. "You coming?"

"In a little bit." She colored her voice with uncertainty. He threw his hands up and entered the bridge. She slipped down to the creek, removed her shoes and socks, and rolled up her pants legs. The water nearly froze her, sneaking up to wet her pant legs. Rocks jabbed her feet, but she slunk across with no big splashes. As she climbed up the bank, briars tore at her, but this ambush would prove oh, so worth it. She crept up to the bridge, and—

"Gaaaaaaaaa!" Garrett leaped at her like a Billy Goats Gruff troll.

She would have fallen backward and rolled down the bank if he hadn't grabbed her and pulled her inside the bridge, screaming and laughing so hard she thought she would die. His strong arms held her tight against him so she could feel his racing heartbeat. Her mirth waned to chuckles the same time his did, drifting away as his hand tilted her face up. At his expression, she forgot to inhale.

If ever a plan backfired, this one—

He brushed her lips with his, then pressed them together, slipping his hands into her hair, holding her face to his until they both were breathless.

She loved the way he held her afterward, his smooth-shaven cheek against hers. But when his hand cupped her chin and began to raise it, she gently pulled away. "Sorry. These bridges post weight limits. They also have kissing limits: one per bridge, maximum. No exceptions."

"Guess we'll have to find another bridge." He sighed deeply. "As soon as possible."

Turning back, she threw a smile over her shoulder. "So get on your bike and ride."

Garrett collected a similar fireworks kiss at Phillips Bridge but decided to forego the privilege at Mecca. Kendra the Adventurer didn't appreciate predictable. Maybe he needed to cool it a little.

"You're still wet from wading, Kendra. It's growing chillier by the moment." He surveyed the rapidly setting sun. "We'd better head back to Rockville."

A distinct look of disappointment passed over her face, and he could hardly contain his exultation. *So you do want me to kiss you. Maybe as much as I want to?*

He almost gave in. Instead, he climbed onto his bike.

When they reached Rockville, he helped her, wet and worn out, load her bike onto her Jeep's carrier. He kissed her quickly on the forehead before she headed home.

Then he walked his bike back to the inn's bike storage room, wolfed down some of the Misses Kincaids' oatmeal cookies, and crashed in his room…only to lie awake, wishing he'd collected his proper bridge toll.

* * *

Checking her messages before bed, Kendra groaned. Roger again.

"I'd really like to see you next weekend. I'm a night owl, so please call me tonight, even if it's late."

His deep voice sounded eager.

She felt nothing.

She still tingled with the taste of Garrett's kisses. True, that last one might have resembled a kiss from her brother—except for Garrett's grip on her shoulder and the dangerous look in his eyes.

Would anything come of this insane relationship?

Even if love grew, would distance dwindle it to nothing?

Whatever happened with Garrett, she now knew nothing would happen with Roger. Not fair to keep him dangling.

She called him. He greeted her with way too much gladness. "Hi, Roger. Sorry to call so late... ."

Chapter 11

Garrett shoveled in Kendra's spinach lasagna. Chase shoveled in her sausage lasagna. Both talked nonstop, using words intelligible only to people who liked comparing photos of dams on cell phones.

Remembering Chase's past reactions to some of her guy friends, she realized she should give thanks they hit it off. She wished, however, they'd include her in the conversation.

Those two probably wouldn't notice if she went to bed—which sounded great. She'd devoted every spare minute to roaming Parke County with Garrett. She yawned. What time did she finish grading papers last night? Two o'clock? Her student pilots tested her patience more than usual. Worst of all, "minor costs" to treat her cabin's logs and correct drainage issues were good for a half-day migraine.

Of course, Terry called. Now interested in another plane, he asked her the exact date she could produce the payment for Ladyhawk. What to do? Her dream still hovered within sight, but would it escape her reach?

Meanwhile, the guys talked on and on.

Hel–lo. I could use some encouragement. Maybe a "thank you" for a two-entrée dinner?

She carried empty plates to the dishwasher. Grabbing a moment when both took a breath, she said, "I have lessons to prepare. Could you please give me a hand?"

"Sure." Garrett rose and brought more dishes to the counter. "You look tired. Maybe we shouldn't have gone to Mansfield today."

"I—I had a wonderful time, though." She tried not to think about his leaving next week.

He reached for her hand. "I did, too."

Suddenly Kendra's everyday pressures didn't seem so tough.

"Hey, guys?"

"Yes, Chase?" At the moment, Kendra wished she'd pushed him out of the cockpit on their last flight.

"I need to talk to you."

"It can't wait?" The half-apologetic, half-ecstatic look in his eye raised red flags.

"I have to confirm by phone tomorrow."

Her world tilted. "You mean—"

"Yeah, Garrett's company has asked me to come for a final interview." His grin consumed his face.

"Awesome!"

How could Garrett knock knuckles with Chase when he'd just sucker-punched her heart? How could she bear the thought of losing them both?

She'd reached her limit.

"That's great," she said wearily. She hugged Chase and made a beeline for her bedroom. She threw herself onto her bed and hugged Grandma's quilts. With a sob, she buried her head in pillows so the guys wouldn't hear her cry.

Garrett shook his head. "Perhaps that wasn't the best timing?"

"Maybe not." Chase still stared down the hall at Kendra's exit route.

Should I follow her? Should Chase? Garrett reproached himself for not seeing her fatigue. After all, he and the teddy bears slept in every morning.

He'd also read an aching good-bye in her eyes, one he couldn't bear to face, either. They should quit pretending and talk. But if she'd already gone to bed—

"I'll knock," Chase offered. "If she wants to talk, she'll talk. If she doesn't, she won't. Either way, you may have to come looking for my remains."

"She may do us both in." Garrett began scraping dishes.

Chase soon returned. "She says she needs sleep. A discussion might go better if we took her to dinner at a nice place in Terre Haute tomorrow night."

Garrett smiled. That sounded more like his Kendra.

His Kendra.

Had he ever thought of a woman that way before?

As they wiped down counters and swept, he marveled that in three short weeks she'd turned his life upside down—in more ways than one. He shuddered, remembering her plane's loops. But he'd brave even that again to keep her in his life.

Afterward, he and Chase shared another offbeat, penetrating Bible study. Tonight they examined Abraham's uncertainties in following God's direction. As they prayed together, Garrett gave thanks for Chase and Hort, two Christian brothers he'd never have met if he hadn't come to Indiana.

Later, as he sat on the Snuggle Bears Inn's front porch, enjoying the crisp autumn night, he thought about their need to talk. He longed to pray with Kendra, too. She'd knelt with him beside Elijah's grave. But shouldn't they pray about their possible future together?

Kendra bought the teal wraparound dress not knowing when she'd wear it. But as her friend Sarah told her during their Facebook chat, every girl should keep a surprise outfit in her closet.

As Kendra and the guys sat at a restaurant's white-clothed table, she blessed her rare extravagance. Garrett had worn a perpetually stunned expression since he'd laid eyes on her. Chase, who'd ditched his jeans for khakis, acted like a grown-up. He didn't even grab the last roll.

Never underestimate the power of a new dress. They weren't ignoring her tonight.

She chitchatted about her work. Garrett shared Elijah Beal research he hadn't mentioned before. Chase told weird dorm stories. After they all agreed the bananas foster had way surpassed their expectations, she sipped coffee and said, "So, Chase, did you confirm your interview at Global?"

"Yes. It's around Thanksgiving."

Kendra struggled to keep trembles—and acid—out of her voice. "Apparently you and Garrett will be seeing a great deal of each other."

"It's not a sure thing, Kendra." Her brother shook his head. "I've applied for two internships in Indy and two in Chicago, too. One way or another, I'll be leaving for a while."

She turned to Garrett. "I assume you wrote him a recommendation?"

"Yes." He met her gaze head-on. "I only endorse the best."

She'd suspected as much. Kendra sipped her coffee again to hide the stupid quiver of her lips. "For the last time, Chase, you won't consider studying for your master's at Rose-Hulman?"

"Not right now." Chase didn't back down. "I don't sense that's where God wants me to go."

"I still don't get that—"

"Do you want to get it, Kendra?"

"Excuse me?" If they hadn't been sitting in a nice, civilized restaurant, she might have thrown the last roll at Chase's nose.

He repeated, "Do you want to be led by God? Like Abraham?"

"Like Elijah Beal?" Garrett raised his chin.

Civilized restaurant or not, she glared at both. "Ganging up on me, are you?"

Chase's face fell. He reached for her hand.

"Why would I want to 'gang up' on you?" He spoke gently.

"You have always been there for me, and I haven't appreciated you enough. I'm not dissing your faith." He leaned forward, funny hair only emphasizing the earnestness of his young face. "If there's anything I've learned from the Bible, it's that God custom designs us. He communicates differently with everyone. I'm sorry if I made it seem as if my way is the only way. I only ask that you open yourself to how He's leading me and consider that He might want a new approach for you, too."

The contagious moisture in his soft hazel eyes wet hers. "I'm sorry I snapped at you. It's just that sometimes, Chase, you're too much. You always have been too bright. Too sweet." She shook her head. "Closer to God than I am…"

Chase turned to Garrett, tilting his hands above his head. "Is my halo lopsided?"

Garrett "straightened" it. "There, that's better."

"Very funny." She let her eyes send them a half glare, half caress.

"God loves you as you are, Sis." Chase rose, leaned down, and planted a kiss on her cheek. "He wants to be your best friend."

He gave her a bony, sideways hug. "I know you want extra time with Garrett tonight, and that's okay. No need to press an eject button. I'm out of here."

He left, long arms swinging like levers.

Kendra wasn't seated straight across from Garrett, so she didn't have to meet his gaze. She only felt it, like a tropical sun, on her cheek and throat.

How could he salvage what he'd hoped would be a special evening? "Want to go for coffee? Is it a double whipped-cream night?"

At least he'd coaxed a faint smile onto Kendra's sad lips.

"Maybe. I'd rather keep walking. Let's wander toward ISU."

They walked past the technology buildings.

Garrett slowed his steps, which he usually didn't do with

Kendra. This evening, though, she ambled along the campus grounds, saying little.

They found a bench near a large, black antique-style clock. A quiet wind wafted a hint of Kendra's spicy perfume his way. She fixed her eyes on the night sky. He fixed his eyes on her.

"So...you think God inserts our names into His smartphone, too? Programs where we should go and what we should do and then sends us e-mails?"

She must have been thinking about this all evening. He said, "No, I don't. That's not what I read in the Bible. He got up close and personal with Abraham."

"Yeah, I remember that. With Abraham. With Moses. With other spiritual superstars. But what about thousands of every-day people?"

"I haven't gone to church or read the Bible as much as you have." Now he wished Chase had stayed. "But from what I understand, the Holy Spirit is with all of us who believe. He directs us."

"You think He directed you to come to Indiana?"

That Garrett could answer. "Yes."

"Why do you think that?"

She stared at him with such intensity that he wondered if she could see through his skin into his soul.

"The more I read Elijah's journal, the more I wanted to read the Bible and hear what God had to say. I prayed, too, and I tried to listen." He hoped he was making sense. "I also wanted to experience where Elijah lived and worked. That's not so strange, is it? That's what I do when I begin any work project. I visit the site."

"So this desire increased as you studied and prayed, and then you took practical action to investigate the idea." She gave a decided nod. "I like that part."

"Yes, although my family didn't see it that way." He grinned wryly. "You'd think I'd planned my vacation in some third world outpost. Plus, they really don't get the spiritual side of this pilgrimage."

"Like the way I reacted to Chase." Her grimace-smile. "I don't want to complicate his spiritual journey—or yours."

"I don't view you as a complication." He took her hand. "In fact, I think you may be an important part of the plan."

Her lips formed soundless words. Then she shook her head. "How can I be part of God's plan for you? You seem to know Him well—like Chase does. I believe Jesus died for my sins. I read Bible-study lessons and pray. But we're different, you and I."

Unease, like early thunder, began a low rumble inside him. "You heard Chase. God speaks to people in different ways. Different can be good."

"As different as we are? Garrett, we live a thousand miles apart."

"I know." He longed to kiss and hold her while he could. He didn't want to talk differences.

Head bowed, she turned her face away. "I want to buy my plane, Garrett. I want to fly it everywhere and come home to my cabin here in Parke County. I—I can't see myself living in your world."

Could he see himself living in hers? *Oh God, help us. Please.*

Her proud shoulders drooped. "What were we thinking? We never should have let things go this far—"

"I disagree." He turned her to him and raised her chin. "I believe you were part of the reason God brought me to Indiana."

"That doesn't make sense."

"I didn't say it made sense. Given the fact we've found each other—"

"Lots of couples 'find each other.' It doesn't always work out. Like my parents." Even in the dimness of the pathway lights, he saw her mouth twist. "For years they took turns dumping Chase and me on our grandparents for temporary stays. Finally Mom and Dad left for good, running in opposite directions."

"I'm so sorry they hurt you." He touched her soft cheek. "Are we like them, Kendra?"

"No." She shook her head slowly, then vehemently. "They are intelligent and educated, but they are not people of faith."

"We are. Plus, we are helping each other grow spiritually."

"Wait." She held up her hand. "Yes, you've pointed me to God. Yes, you and Chase model a faith I envy. But me? Help you grow spiritually? I don't think so."

"You're wrong, there." He leaned toward her, shaping every word carefully. "You've traipsed around with me on this ridiculous—I'm quoting my parents, here—pilgrimage, when any other woman would have found better things to do than hear about Elijah Beal. You've listened to me mull over my beliefs and asked honest questions. You've helped point me to God. I want you to keep doing that." He took a deep breath. "So would you pray with me about our future?"

Her face shone pale in the starlight. "It will take a miracle for our relationship to survive."

"Yes, it will. If it grows, we'll know for sure God has brought us together." He took both her hands. "Pray with me, Kendra?"

She nodded slightly. "You first."

He didn't bow his head or close his eyes because he wanted to look at the sky. "Lord, You are the Creator of the universe. You made the stars. They move at Your direction. You made Kendra and me. Please guide us, too. Amen."

At his words, she raised her head, her gaze sweeping the sky. "Lord, as much time as I've spent sitting in a church pew, I should know You better. Please help Garrett and me understand what You want for us. Amen."

He wanted to cheer. He wanted to give her the kiss she couldn't forget in a million years, but contented himself with clasping her to him, hoping the perfect moment would follow soon.

The stretched-wire tenseness he'd felt in her earlier had relaxed. Just as he reached for her face, she sprang up, almost under his nose.

"Yay! Now we can enjoy the weekend at Turkey Run, not waste it pretending and beating around the bush."

Actually, he'd been trying to forget about Turkey Run... .

She grabbed his hand. "I feel like walking."

Apparently she felt like jogging.

Soon they arrived at the student union. White-gold streams of water sprayed from the fountain in front of the portico, illuminating the night like arced liquid spotlights. He stopped a few paces away. Despite the chilly night, she walked to the edge and wiggled her fingers in the tumbling water, giggling like a child. Gleams and glimmers found Kendra, touching her blue dress, her joyous face, the coppery curls cascading down her back.

She turned, a wicked gleam in her eye.

He stared her down. "Get me wet, and I'll kiss you in front of God and everybody."

She filled both hands and flung them at him.

Dripping, he grabbed her and gave her the knock-your-socks-off kiss he'd been dreaming of all evening.

It was, after all, the perfect moment.

Chapter 12

After Garrett studied the tent instructions a few minutes, he surprised Kendra by setting it up perfectly.

"I *am* an engineer, after all." He gave her his insulted look—which Kendra thought was cute.

He and Chase quickly raised the other tent and micro-organized the campsite. *Fine. Go ahead, you two, invent a robot that carries firewood.*

Finished with her tasks, Kendra went next door to Rose and Al Hammond's enormous RV and collaborated about meals with Hort and Rose. They loved camp cooking, so Kendra agreed to buy groceries as needed. She also volunteered herself and the guys for cleanup.

"Thanks a lot, Kendra." Chase grouched, upon hearing her arrangements.

"Rose sent over chocolate chip, macadamia nut cookies." Kendra opened a yellowed Tupperware container.

Her brother grabbed two. With one bite, his eyes glazed over. He took three more.

"Not such a bad idea?" Kendra grinned.

"Even better than my cookies."

"That's saying something." She never could make them as yummy as his. "Save room, Chase. Hort's making chili, and Rose, campfire peach cobbler and ice cream."

"Do we have time for a hike first?" Chase shifted from one big tennis-shoed foot to the other. "You have to see the suspension bridge, Garrett, and you won't believe Trail 3's terrain."

"Sounds great." Garrett took Kendra's hand.

"They'll expect us around 6:30, so if we return on Trail 10, we can make it without pushing." She tried not to think how she would miss his strong hand holding hers. *Don't fixate on his leaving. Enjoy him now, this moment.*

They walked past the inn, pool, and nature center before encountering Sugar Creek.

"Nice." Garrett surveyed the steel cable and wooden bridge anchored into huge cliff-like shelves of sandstone, stretching high above smooth, patchwork-colored water. He read aloud the black-and-gold wooden sign on the bridge's tall cement edifice: Rocky Hollow-Falls Canyon Nature Preserve.

"One of my favorite places in the world." This bridge always made her feel like skipping. On the other side, she clomped down wooden steps to the water's surface and walked back into the cavernous rock overhang. "When we came here as kids, I pretended I was a cavewoman."

"She dragged me home by my hair." Chase yanked his curls and made an awful face.

"How she abuses you." Garrett grinned. As they followed the rugged trail through deepening woods into gullies full of ferns, then misty, mossy canyons with streams at the bottom, he shivered. "Whoa, did we change continents? All these weird rock formations, and the temperature must be twenty degrees colder down here."

"This area's called the Icebox." Kendra shivered, too, and they snuggled together in another enormous cave-like hollow. "Feels wonderful during mid-July, but a little chilly in October."

"We'll soon be climbing out of here," Chase consoled them. "Remember the ladders?"

"Ladders?" Garrett shot Kendra a what-did-you-get-me-into-now look.

"They're just wooden ladders we climb in order to continue the trail." She shrugged. "No biggie."

"Right," he snorted later as they took a more relaxed Trail 10 back to the suspension bridge, Chase running ahead like a curious hound. "You didn't tell me we'd go rock climbing. Or that I'd slip and nearly break my neck. 'No biggie.' " He imitated Kendra in a high falsetto. "As if those ladders made it so easy."

"They were a little slick," Kendra admitted. "The mist condenses on them."

He looked heavenward, as if praying. "Just once, I'd like you to be predictable—"

"You would?" She cast a glance at him.

"No, I wouldn't." He stopped, drew her into a rocky nook, and pressed his lips against hers, hard.

Thrills of joy and pain spiraled together down her body. *Don't go, Garrett. Stay with me.*

His mouth worked as he held her face in his hands. Desire. She saw it in his eyes. If she manipulated him, he might stay.

No. Not that way. Not good for either of them.

She placed a finger on his mouth. "We're due to sample Hort's chili in fifteen minutes."

He nodded slowly. "We'd better go, or Chase will eat it all."

She laughed, her eyes tearing up. His strong hand grasped hers again, and they walked resolutely back to the campsite.

"God puts on a real show, doesn't He?" Hort leaned back into his camp chair, scanning the night sky. "I think He enjoys planning a different one every night."

Garrett raised his eyes. "I've never seen a moon quite like that." The full translucent globe glimmered behind spiky black tree silhouettes, sheer fringed clouds draped across it.

"Makes me think of the pearl of great price in the Bible." Kendra, beside him, spoke in a low voice. "If I found a pearl like that, I'd give everything I had to buy it."

"Even your airplane money?" Chase teased.

Garrett saw the smile disappear as if she'd wiped it off with her paper napkin. She said nothing. Why did Chase remind her that her dream might not happen—at least, not soon?

Garrett tried to salvage the moment. "That's the best peach cobbler I ever ate," he told Rose, sitting across from them.

"Sure is." Hort waved a spoon to emphasize his opinion.

She beamed. "Baking it in the dutch oven over campfire coals gives it that special flavor."

"You'll never eat anything better." Al patted his wife's hand.

Chase, who seemed to realize he'd upset his sister, told his funniest stories. Hort entertained them with festival tales, including one about a girl, a Miss Blueberry at the Plymouth, Indiana, Blueberry Festival, who worked her way up the corporate ladder. Upon returning to her hometown for the festival a decade later, she proceeded to win the blueberry pie-eating contest.

"Blue as a Smurf afterward. Good thing she'd greased up with Vaseline beforehand and most of it came off. She was supposed to be in a wedding!"

He also told them about a skinny guy who bet his friends he could eat five elephant ears at one sitting—and did.

"Made a pile of money that night," Hort chuckled.

"I don't approve of gambling." Rose crossed her arms.

"I don't, either." Hort's grin didn't fade. "I'm not talking about him. I'm talking about me. Once he proved he could eat five at once, his friends tried to beat him."

Kendra giggled. Her smile and hair competed with the embers for sheer glow. Garrett wanted to take that glow home to color his drab, precise world.

But he couldn't. At least, not yet.

He reached for her hand. He'd soon return to the rhythms of

the city, the pushing pace that dictated the beat of his heart and brain. Garrett inhaled slowly. Exhaled. Lay back in his chair.

For now, he'd enjoy good friends in Christ around a crackling campfire, the glimmering stars, and Kendra—the woman who, in his eyes, rivaled them as the loveliest spectacle God ever designed.

"Are you sure you don't want to canoe with us this morning?" Snarfing down another of Rose's to-die-for apple pecan muffins, Kendra hoped Chase would say yes.

Hunched over their picnic table, he nodded. "Hort, Al, and I are going fishing. Rose offered to do a fish fry tonight if we catch the bluegills."

Chase grabbed his fishing pole and ambled to the Hammonds' RV, whistling. She marveled how her brother, impossible to awaken at home, popped out of his sleeping bag at the crack of dawn when they camped.

Garrett, too. Sleeping in the tiny yellow dome tent, she awoke when the *zzzip!* of their tent flap and murmuring voices interrupted her dreams. Watching Garrett's tall figure return, she didn't mind. An early start meant more time with him today.

He pulled out his phone.

"Are you checking your e-mail? The baseball play-off scores?" She tried not to feel annoyed.

"Not this weekend. I want to read my Bible."

"Good idea." She pulled out her phone, too. While most of the campground slept, in the brand-new crispness of the fall morning, they read together.

This the first time I've read the Bible with a man.

She hoped it wouldn't be the last.

Kendra suggested walking through Narrows Covered Bridge, which crossed Sugar Creek at their launching spot, before they began their canoe trip in earnest. To her surprise, Garrett vetoed the idea.

"I have my reasons. We'll check out Narrows Bridge sometime this weekend."

His provocative smile liquefied her knees. *Bridge? What bridge?*

So they loaded the canoe and donned life jackets, Garrett securing his glasses with a head strap. They let the strong current, created by plentiful fall rains, propel them downstream as she steered from the back. Garrett's stroke gradually improved, and he no longer slapped the water with his paddle. They synchronized with less instruction from her, which made for a happier man and a fun Indian summer afternoon floating along a vivid wilderness landscape.

Garrett seemed to enjoy analyzing details of the suspension bridge's construction from the water. After they checked out Cox Ford Bridge, they stretched out on a sandbar for a brief rest in the golden sunshine—good preparation, Kendra thought, for possibly more challenging waters ahead.

From the canoe's front, Garrett watched the swirling water. Just once, he'd like to impress Kendra, to look as if he knew what he was doing.

But that moment wasn't now.

"Maybe you'd better let me paddle alone in this section of the creek." Kendra had left her soft, womanly persona behind on Cox Ford Bridge. Now she wore her professional mask as she expertly dipped her paddle in the increasingly fast-running water. "We're approaching an island. They can cause tricky shifts in the current, especially since the water level is up. No biggie, though. We'll be out of here in no time."

Despite his frustration, Garrett cooperated, notifying her of deceptive rocks in the water, watching more and more white, rushing ridges emerge from the creek's surface. Rapids? In Indiana? He cast occasional glances over his shoulder to watch Kendra. Her eyes arrowhead sharp, the muscles in her arms working, she slid their canoe toward and away from the shoreline in a wilderness choreography that took his breath away.

Suddenly Kendra dug frantically with her paddle and yelled at the top of her lungs. He grabbed his—but the canoe crashed into something big under the water, then tipped crazily. A wall of icy, gray-green water smacked his face, filled his nose, pressed his torso down against a bruising rocky bottom.

Chapter 13

"Garrett!" The current rammed the half-submerged canoe against Kendra, flattening her against a jutting boulder. She struggled to find her footing in the frigid water. Pain shot through the left side of her rib cage when she inhaled, but she yelled and yelled for him.

No one. Nothing.

You had to show off again, didn't you, Kendra? Took it a little too far this time.

Icy water chilled her body, but a flush of shame burned her cheeks. They should have portaged rather than paddled through those rapids.

Where was Garrett? Was he all right? She shouted once more. A wave of panic nearly drowned her until she reminded herself that going to pieces would not do Garrett—or her—any good. He'd worn a life jacket and no doubt was wet but unharmed. The current had carried him farther downstream. Even now, he might be walking onshore, returning to the site of their mishap—ready to wring her neck... .

The current tried to wrench the paddle she clutched. She

guarded it fiercely. Time to forget couldas and shouldas. She would empty and right the canoe then search Sugar Creek until she found Garrett. Grasping the protruding side of the canoe, she grunted with pain as she tried to jiggle it.

It didn't budge.

She couldn't budge. The canoe's bottom, forced by the current, loomed in her face, pressing, forcing her against the rocks. With her shoulders and one arm, she fought it. The boulder behind her pushed stony knobs into her legs, her back. *I can't move it. Harder to breathe…What will I do?*

Keep moving. That's what you'll do. She wiggled her toes and occasionally flapped her arms and legs underwater to keep circulation flowing. If only the Indian summer sun heating her head could warm her heavy, numb body.

Edging the canoe bottom away from her face with her shoulders, Kendra fought to reach inside. No backpack. No cell.

She couldn't do this alone. If Garrett was still floating downriver, other canoeists would paddle this way. They'd seen several earlier. Surely they would come… .

The water chilled her as if it flowed from a glacier. She shivered uncontrollably. *It's only October, Kendra. Don't let your imagination carry you away.*

Despite efforts to condense her emotions into calm wait-for-help mode, a tiny inner current of fear eddied in her mind, then her heart, threatening to grow into a whirlpool. *What happened to Garrett? What if no one ever comes—*

"Kendra? Kendra!"

"Garrett!" Warm tears spurted down her cold face.

"Where are you?" He sounded some distance away.

She took as deep a breath as she could and shouted, "Upstream! I'm trapped!"

Hearing his footsteps crash through the underbrush, she yelled several times, despite pain. Straining, she finally spotted him. "Here!"

He'd never looked better—though his left eye already was turning purple and a cut on his cheek was bleeding. Garrett plunged into the water, fighting the current until he stood beside her. "Are you all right?"

"Probably bruised a rib. Your eye—"

"I'm fine. Let's pull you out." He grabbed the canoe. "Whoa, the current *is* strong here."

"If we push together, I think we can manage." She added, "I can make it to shore on my own. When I get free, grab the canoe, okay?"

"The canoe?" He looked at her as if she'd lost her mind. "You're worried about the *canoe*?"

"We'd rather canoe than walk all the way to the pickup point, right?"

He nodded. "All right, let's do this."

With the determination in his voice, she felt fresh strength stir in her frozen arms. "Okay, one. Two. Three."

They tried it once. Twice. Several times. Finally, together they wrenched the canoe loose, and she wriggled free. Clutching her paddle, she made for shore. She dragged herself up onto the muddy bank and watched as he edged the canoe to land. When the front neared the shore, she rose to grab it.

"Leave it alone, Kendra," he ordered. "I'll pull it out."

Her hackles rose at his tone, but she realized she was weaving from side to side. She dropped back onto the bank, shivering, miniature waterfalls streaming from her soppy clothes and shoes.

He managed to push the canoe ashore and flopped beside her. He cupped her face in his hands as if he couldn't believe she was real. "I searched and searched." He raised his face to the sky. "Thank You, God, that I found her."

Covering her bruised side with her arm, she leaned against him, feeling small—and about as smart—as a tadpole. "I'm so sorry, Garrett. This was all my fault."

"Shhh." He laid a finger on her lips. "None of that. You're exhausted. We need to dry out before attempting to paddle again."

He lay back against a leafless tree trunk, holding her as

carefully as if she were a rose. The sun's friendly rays wrapped them in sleepy blankets of warmth, and she closed her eyes.

"There it is. Jackson Covered Bridge." Kendra, sitting in the front, didn't turn because of her rib, but he heard the smile in her voice. "Looks like other canoeists are waiting, too. One of them will have a cell we can use to call the shuttle."

Garrett, lifting the paddle with tired arms, breathed a sigh of relief. After their nap, he'd carried the canoe past the rapids. Fortunately, the creek broadened as hilly forests morphed into flat fields, calming its waters. With Kendra's guidance, he'd navigated without hitting the shore too many times.

Floating to the landing, they must look even worse than he felt. Spectators raised their heads and stared at them like cows.

"Need help?" called a college-aged guy onshore.

"Yes, thanks." Kendra had said her rib only hurt when she laughed or coughed, but he noticed she exited the canoe cautiously. "We hit a boulder and capsized."

Their Good Samaritans grabbed the canoe and landed it. Garrett waded ashore and thanked them.

He and Kendra did a slow walk-through of the Jackson Covered Bridge—named after President Andrew Jackson by J. Daniels, who built it right before the Civil War.

The shuttle soon arrived. Their helpful new friends loaded Kendra's canoe onto its trailer and then onto her Jeep when they arrived back at their starting point.

Garrett pulled his phone from under the passenger seat. "Let's stop by the nearest emergency room and have your rib checked out."

She crossed her arms. "Let's check your eye out, too."

"It's only a black eye—"

"Mine's only a bruised rib. Even if it's broken—I've broken a rib before—they can't treat it any differently than I will."

"Except they'd give you pain medicine."

"I wouldn't take it, anyway." She threw the Jeep into gear.

Why am I not surprised? He dropped his head back and closed his eyes.

"I'll pick up some medicine for us at the campground store." She peeled out, as usual.

Somehow, the sound of thrown gravel reassured him. She must feel okay.

When Kendra started driving like normal people, then perhaps he should worry.

"Kendra, what did you *do* to him?" Chase stared at Garrett as they returned to the campsite. "I shouldn't have let you two go without me."

As usual, her brother was more accurate than he knew. *I should never have attempted those rapids.* Aloud, she said, "We hit a boulder, and the boulder won."

"She's more hurt than I am." Garrett led her to the chaise lounge. "Here, rest. Where's a blanket? Her clothes are still damp."

Chase dove into his tent, retrieved a sports blanket, and spread it around her. "What's the matter, Kendra?"

"I bruised a rib." She tried not to wince. "No biggie."

Garrett folded his arms. "I'm learning to distrust that phrase."

"Anyway, all's well that ends well." She pointed to a camp chair. "*You* need to rest. Garrett rescued me and paddled us down to Jackson Bridge, though he was hurt, too. Fortunately, some other canoeists helped us land the canoe and load up, and here we are."

Garrett bent and dropped a kiss on the top of her head.

"Think I'll take a shower and rest in my tent until supper," he said. "See you under the stars."

Garrett surprised Kendra by eating bluegills that night. She couldn't recall seeing him eat anything with this much gusto.

"Ever had 'em before?" Hort passed the platter to him again.

"Never."

"Putting them away pretty good, aren't you?"

Garrett forked more crisp batter-fried fish onto his plate. "Canoeing works up an appetite."

Especially if you're trying to keep from drowning. A fresh wave of shame rolled over her.

"Plus, these looked too delicious to pass up."

A beaming Rose said, "Have more fried potatoes."

"You're spoiling me big-time."

Tonight around the fire, Kendra snuggled close, too grateful for their safety to pretend she didn't care deeply about him. Though careful, Garrett held her as if he'd never let her go.

The fire faded into an indistinct glow. Kendra caught herself halfway through a snore. Rising a little unsteadily, she said, "I think I'm done for the night."

"You don't want to sit around the campfire?" Chase acted as if she'd uttered blasphemy. "You don't want *s'mores*?"

She felt rather than saw Garrett's pleading eyes and considered the positives of staying:

S'more yummy campfire food of the gooey, chocolate, and marshmallow persuasion.

S'more delicious warmth, comforting her hurting bones.

S'more of the fairy-tale sky above them, where she felt she could pick stars like flowers.

S'more of Garrett's strong, gentle arm around her, the tiny, secret kisses he would breathe into her hair... .

A person would be crazy not to want s'more.

He'd never been a fan of restrooms down the hall, let alone down the road, but Garrett had willed himself to adjust. If he could live with two hundred teddy bears for three weeks, he could handle this.

Especially if a trip to brush his teeth morphed into an opportunity to walk with Kendra. Hey, he'd take it. The past week, his inner clock ticked louder and louder, never letting him forget that soon he would have to leave her... .

The postmidnight campground had quieted considerably,

and right now he held her hand in his, reveling in the soft glimmers of the stars overhead and those in her eyes.

"Maybe I won't have to wait for a free sink." Kendra sounded wistful.

Ridiculous that separating at different doors should seem so difficult. It gave him a minisense of what the next day or two held for them.

He'd just stuck his toothbrush into his mouth when an unearthly scream nearly sent it down his throat.

"EEEEEEEEEEeeeeeeeeeeeeeeeee!"

His feet carried him out the door into the women's side, where Kendra, white as the toothpaste mustache smeared above her mouth, quaked like a sapling in a storm.

"Kendra, what's wrong?"

Hand shaking, she pointed to a stall.

"Did someone hurt you?" Everything in him wanted to crush her attacker.

She choked, weeping anew. He slid between her and the stall, ready to battle with his bare hands.

"Locked?" he mouthed.

She shook her head, her eyes black with terror.

He crouched, gathering strength for the knockout punch. No feet visible on the floor, but some creeps might pounce from the toilet itself. Garrett smacked the stall door with his fist.

The attacker stood on the toilet seat, all right.

He measured about three inches in height.

The wet mouse froze then hopped to the floor.

Kendra, behind Garrett, let loose another bloodcurdling scream then dashed for the exit. Garrett followed—

Only to look down the barrel of a gun wielded by a very large, distinctly unfriendly man.

"Mister, just what do you think you're doin'?"

One thirty in the morning. Garrett didn't bother to unzip the tent quietly. Chase apparently had slumbered peacefully while Garrett risked life and limb rescuing his sister from killer vermin.

"But he was *wet*," she'd tried to explain. "Those horrible beady eyes, and—and—he w-wiggled his whiskers at me!" He'd cautiously—because the guy with the gun still appeared to question Garrett's story—tried to soothe her.

Finally Kendra's other would-be rescuer returned to his RV, swearing at idiots who disturbed God-fearing people's sleep. Garrett inspected the men's restroom and stood guard so Kendra could brush her teeth, walking her back to her tent to protect her from other homicidal mice. With the night's excitement—not to mention their earlier adventures on and in Sugar Creek—Garrett wanted nothing more than to tunnel into his sleeping bag. He longed to redream the quiet, starry joy of the campfire, the tenderness of Kendra close to him, his head resting on her hair.

Who would have thought she could emit a sound akin to that of a freaked-out fire engine?

Chase said, "She can yell when she wants to, right?"

"*You* heard her?"

"Sure. Who didn't?" Chase yawned. "But I knew it was just her critter scream."

"Her what?"

"Her critter scream. Not that Kendra scares easily. She faked pulling a gun on a guy who tried to burglarize her ISU office. I think he was actually glad when Campus Safety picked him up."

Despite what he'd endured the past two hours, Garrett believed it. "What kinds of critters make her scream like that?"

"Well, mice. You already knew that."

Yes he did.

"She isn't afraid of snakes or spiders. But centipedes and millipedes, especially in the shower, will send her into the stratosphere."

"Anything else?"

"Nothing I can remember." Chase yawned again and turned

over. "Thanks for taking care of her. I've done it since I was a little kid."

Garrett yearned to sleep, but his mind stayed awake trying to figure out what other Kendra-surprises might lurk in his future.

No wonder Chase wanted to leave home.

Chapter 14

"I'm sorry." Kendra, sweet and big-eyed, mouthed her apology to Garrett over her brother's head, while Chase focused on Hort's fluffy buttermilk pancakes.

Garrett opened his hands and shrugged with a smile, as if to say, "It was nothing."

Actually, remembering the critter commotion, his stomach so swelled with swallowed laughter that he excused himself on pretense of a restroom break and vented his yuks several campsites down. Returning to the picnic table, he now had room for a plateful of pancakes.

Garrett had dreamed of worshipping in an authentic log cabin during his trip to Indiana, and now he could. He, Kendra, Chase, Hort, and the Hammonds set out to attend the service in Turkey Run's log church. Holding his hand, Kendra said little as they walked. A wrinkle formed between her eyebrows, a sure sign her inner wheels were turning.

He said, "You're quiet today."

She glanced around at the richly colored wooded arch through which they strolled. "I was thinking about what it would be like to walk through the forest to church every Sunday, whether it rained, snowed, or flooded."

"Elijah did a lot of that. Nothing seemed to keep him from worshipping God."

She nodded, her face thoughtful. Not only did she understand his passion for Elijah's life story, she had begun thinking about her own faith in similar terms. He gave thanks they could share this worship experience together.

Soon they spotted the little building. Several other worshippers entered its heavy wooden doors.

Garrett walked to a corner and ran his hands over the cabin's wide boards, sawn from giant hardwoods that once covered most of Indiana. He noted how they fitted together perfectly, once caulked with dried mud, now with mortar. No nails. "I can see Elijah worshipping here."

They entered and sat on the plain wooden benches. A fortyish man who introduced himself as Pastor Cody Rawlins led the singing, as well as giving the sermon. He wore an Indianapolis Colts sweatshirt, ripped jeans, and an earring. He played a mean guitar.

Did Charles Wesley ever, in his wildest dreams, picture such a twangy, folksy version of his hymn "O for a Thousand Tongues"? Pastor Cody led other hymns Garrett had never heard that almost demanded toe-tapping: songs about calling rolls in heaven, flying away, and everlasting arms. Everyone seemed to know them well, even singing harmony. Not the kind of music Garrett listened to, but their contagious joy infected him, and he found himself belting out the chorus of the last song: *Leaning, leaning, safe and secure from all alarms; leaning, leaning, leaning on the everlasting arms.*

Kendra's husky voice sang beside him, and he realized that today, of all days, they needed the everlasting arms. With all their challenges, only God could hold them together.

The pastor didn't mince words during his sermon. He spoke about David's Psalm 39: "Show me, Lord, my life's end and

the number of my days; let me know how fleeting my life is…
Lord, what do I look for? My hope is in You."

"Where do we get off, thinking we're in control?" Pastor Cody's Adam's apple bobbed. "Even if we don't read the Bible, one look at Turkey Run State Park, one night under the stars and moon should tell us He's in charge here. The sooner we figure that out, the better, because as David said, our lives won't last forever."

Garrett marveled at the mindlessness of his earlier years. He thought of his grandfather's late legacy of faith, and Elijah Beal's powerful witness through his journal, more than a century and a half after his death. He thought of Hort's and Chase's instruction, Kendra's questions.

Thank you, Jesus, that You've brought me this far. Thank You for helping me figure it out.

"You don't have to break camp today. I'll do it."

Chase's unexpected offer after their lunchtime sandwiches brought a smile to Kendra's lips. "That's really sweet of you."

He gave her a gentle hug. "Consider it very late compensation for having sprayed your prom date with the garden hose."

She turned to Garrett. "Want to take another canoe ride?"

She giggled at the way he froze. "Just kidding. How about a hike?"

"I would like that. Are you sure you feel like doing something that strenuous?"

"We can take it slow and rest a lot." She wanted to drain the tension that tried to dog the day.

He touched her cheek. "Let's not forget Narrows Bridge."

With the look he gave her, she didn't think she'd forget.

Hort refrained from giving Kendra his usual bear hug because of her sore rib. "Take care, Red Wonder," he whispered in her ear. "Remember what I said. God's got great things in store for you."

Garrett's eyes looked moist as Hort hugged him, too. The

elephant ear maker said, "Let me know what you think of that passage in First John, all right?"

"I'll probably e-mail you every day."

More hugs from the Hammonds and a bag of cookies for the hike.

No more good-byes. Kendra wanted to turn and run. *I don't want to think about good-bye.*

Holding hands, they crossed the suspension bridge and wandered through trees so colorful Garrett said he felt as if he'd discovered an autumn Eden. They hiked through rugged gorges, some narrow, some big and resonant as amphitheaters, sheer sandstone cliffs rising around them like cathedral walls. They waded rushing, noisy little streams at the bottom of canyons and viewed glacial potholes like the Punch Bowl. Kendra stood under massive rock overhangs so Garrett could take photos of her to convince his friends in DC that Indiana wasn't all flat.

However, he refused to climb the ladders again. "Once was enough."

She lost track of how far they hiked. But her legs didn't. "I feel like I can't take another step," she said as shadows lengthened.

"Um, I don't think I can carry you piggyback to Narrows Bridge."

"Let's rest then hike back. We'll drive to the bridge."

"That's the smartest thing you've said all day."

Kendra eased the Jeep from the parking lot.

Garrett, who had started to doze off, sat up straight. *She didn't peel out?* He wanted to say, "Kendra, what's wrong?"

She drooped as she drove. He eyed her the rest of the way. Hopefully, she'd feel better after they ate.

They pulled up near the bridge just as the sun waved hello to the horizon. He opened the backpack and handed her a peanut butter and jelly sandwich as they walked to a grassy spot beside it. The air was growing chilly. He didn't mind; they'd keep each other warm. Too ravenous to talk, they demolished two sandwiches apiece, apples, trail mix, and the last of Rose's cookies.

A little color had returned to Kendra's face, along with her smile. "That hit the spot."

He slipped an arm around her, and they sat, watching Sugar Creek mirror the glories of the evening sky. He wondered when he would feel this content, this blessed, again.

She surprised him by saying she wanted to apologize.

"For what?"

"For—for acting like a fool over that stupid rodent." Kendra covered her reddening face with her hand.

He almost said, *But I enjoyed the show.*

He amended his words—"I was glad to help."

"It's just that I *hate* mice! Chase and Grandpa used to think it was funny to hide dead ones in my room."

He crossed his heart. "I will never, ever do that. No mice. Dead or alive."

"Good." She sighed with relief. "Now let me finish apologizing before I talk myself out of it."

"What do you mean?

Her smile fled. "I didn't act responsibly when we went canoeing. With the water that high, we shouldn't have tried to shoot the rapids. We should have portaged around them."

"You're still worried about that? You're the one with the hurt rib—"

"You're the one with the purple eye."

"It makes me look manly. It will document my wounded-hero stories to tell around the watercooler."

No smile from her. "You could have been hurt badly, even drowned, if you'd smacked your head on a rock. All because I wanted to do the exciting thing, not the wise thing."

He held her downcast face in his hand. "Exciting is who you are."

* * *

At his words, she didn't dare look up.

Slowly he raised her chin to meet his eyes. "I like you that way. I want to learn to love you, Kendra."

"I…I want to learn to love you, too." She battled her tears. "But—"

"But what?"

"The odds are so small that we'll make it—"

"So let's beat the odds." His hand dropped. He sounded almost businesslike. "Let's start by setting a time to see each other again. How about Thanksgiving? Chase's interview is scheduled around then, anyway."

"You mean, spend Thanksgiving in Washington?"

"Don't make it sound like Saturn."

She couldn't imagine not baking a turkey and pumpkin pies in her own log cabin kitchen. Still, if Chase went without her… "What about your family? Have you discussed this with them yet?"

"No. But Mother enjoys hosting guests for holiday dinners. You and Chase can stay at my apartment so you won't have to put on your company manners all the time."

"That might prove a real strain." She was only half kidding.

"I know." Those blue, blue eyes looked far too wise.

She stuck out her tongue.

"I have asked my parents to meet us tomorrow for coffee when we land."

Her lungs flattened. "You're kidding."

His eyebrows crunched over his nose. "If we're serious about cultivating a relationship, shouldn't I introduce you to them?"

"But you said they acted as if Indiana were a third world outpost." Indignation and fear bubbled in her stomach. "What—what if they don't like me?"

"They're excellent judges of character. They chose me for their son, didn't they?"

She rolled her eyes. "Obviously they forgot to take humility into consideration."

"Obviously. But considering all my other outstanding traits—"

"Keep it up. I may change my mind about this serious relationship thing."

His hand cupped her chin again. "You wouldn't do that, would you?"

No, no, she wouldn't do that, and he knew it. Rats. She didn't like this loss-of-control feeling... .

"So you'll have coffee with us at the airport?"

How could someone with a black eye look so irresistible? "All right. I'll try to behave."

"Just be yourself."

Right. Being herself didn't always work in academia or new social settings.

He continued, as if he'd already crossed that item off his list. "Frequent communication will be vital for us. Agreed?"

"Um, agreed." She felt as if she were on the receiving end of an interoffice memo.

"So may I call you every night?" Suddenly he sounded as if they were in high school.

She laughed, trying to absorb his schizo CEO/boyfriend persona. "Of course. Call me every night. Call me every morning." A surge of yearning almost broke her voice. "Call me as often as you want."

He ran his finger down her cheek. "Then I'd be on the phone with you every single moment."

"And your point is?" She tried to grin.

He pulled her to him. "Someday," he said softly, "we'll spend much more time together than on the phone."

She drew back and searched his face. "You really believe that, don't you?"

"I do. I believe God sent me here to develop spiritually. And to find you. Which brings me to another point—the most important one." He took her hands. "Will you pray for us every day, Kendra?"

"I have been praying." She'd never prayed about a guy before, but since their talk at ISU, she'd spent more time in prayer, much of it for Garrett and their future.

"I want to share what I've been studying in the Bible, too." He paused. "I *need* to hear your questions, Kendra. They help me think things through."

"I—I should study more. Hopefully, this can be a growing time for both of us." *But why does growing have to be so hard?*

"God will help us." He squeezed her hand. "I think it's time to walk the bridge."

He acted as if this bridge presented something more special than the other thirty he'd explored. Entering the dusky structure, hand in hand with Garrett, she scanned the struts, painted white halfway up for visibility, the rafters, the stout oak floor. Sweet sadness welled up in her. This would be the last covered bridge they'd walk together for a while.

Tonight of all nights, she expected a kiss she could replay when she missed the taste of his lips, the strong warmth of his arms.

They'd already walked halfway across the bridge, and he was still shining his stupid little flashlight on the sides, the ceiling, making notes on his stupid phone. Garrett usually didn't wait this long to kiss her; why the delay?

"You've told me stories about the bridges we've visited together. I thought I would share one tonight."

This was so not going the way she'd expected.

He continued as if following a script. "This was the first bridge Joseph Britton built back in 1882—"

Yippee for Joseph. She already knew this, and she was still waiting for her kiss.

"But while he was building it, his wife passed away, and he was left alone and hurting."

She hadn't heard that part. Half of her felt sorry for the

poor man. The other half asked, *"Garrett, why on earth are you telling me this?"*

Garrett stopped, pocketed his flashlight and phone, and then turned to her. The final rays of sunset shone into the dark interior through the open windows, lighting his face. "One day, when he was feeling loneliest, a woman who lived down the road walked here to watch the bridge go up. That woman became his wife."

The *W* word. Kendra caught her breath. They'd discussed a relationship, a serious relationship, but—

"You came to me at one of the loneliest times of my life, Kendra. My family and friends didn't understand the profound change in my life, how I felt about God. But you listened. You questioned, but you understood. I wish we could fast-forward time and experience so I could ask you right now to be my wife. But neither of us are ready for that."

She knew he spoke the truth, but her foolish heart sank lower than the bridge floor.

"I want to make you a promise." Garrett took her hand and, to her utter amazement, sank to the bridge floor. "Someday, God willing, I will bring you here again, and I will ask you to marry me, to be my wife and partner for the rest of our lives."

"And someday, God willing," Kendra answered, "I will say yes."

It was all she could do to keep from shouting it till the bridge echoed a hundred yeses.

He rose, clasped her in his arms, and gave her the kiss she could replay a thousand times and never wear out the thrill.

Chapter 15

If he hadn't fallen for Kendra before, he would have during the plane ride back to DC.

She looked like a model, wearing a sleek sage-green pants outfit, her coppery waves captured in a hairdo she told him was a french roll. He thought her lovely even after the rapids dunked her into Sugar Creek, but today he could have spent the entire trip just looking at her.

As they sailed through acres of sky and grayish-white cotton-ball clouds, he tried to steer the conversation away from their dreaded good-bye.

Kendra attempted her own method of distraction. Grinning, she eased the control wheel back. "Matthew. Mark."

The plane arced upward.

"Luke. John." He tried to keep a nonchalant expression. "Acts. Romans. Hey, you have any barf bags handy?"

She paused. "You wouldn't."

"Not intentionally. But you never know."

The plane magically settled into a level path. "You're no fun."

"Sorry. I just happen to like living right side up." He laughed.

She did, too.

He watched her capable hands steer and check instruments, her feet move the rudder as if she were part of the plane. "You really do love this thing, don't you?"

She stroked the yoke as if it were her child's head. "Yes, I do. I can't wait to call this bird my own."

"I love my work, too. Somehow, though, I don't bond with it as you do with your plane."

"Ladyhawk's much more to me than a machine." Kendra ran her finger along the control panel. "She takes me places I only dreamed of going when I was a kid. I'm not sure I could make it without her. When we're soaring up here, I feel close to God."

He was beginning to understand, though flying in the tiny plane still made him feel close to God only in a passenger-on-the-*Titanic* sense.

Does she care about me as much as she does Ladyhawk? The thought popped up in his mind like an ad on a computer monitor. He closed it. A little early in their relationship to ask questions like that.

Does she care about God as much as she does flying? Bigger question. Even more important. But did he have the right to ask? He'd left his work and lifestyle for three weeks. What if God wanted a change—a big change—in his life?

"You're quiet." Her scrutiny rested on controls and the sky, but he felt her focus on him.

He paused. "I was thinking that we have a lot to learn about each other, about our connections to God. I'm glad we're studying First John with Hort and Chase online. They say that book talks about God's love."

"A subject I need to study. Looking at what He's made, I've always believed in God's love." Her lips continued to smile, but her hands tightened on the wheel. "Sometimes, though, my parents' leaving Chase and me makes it hard to feel that."

"I never had to deal with that kind of hurt. I wish you didn't."

Garrett gently rubbed her arm, feeling the tension relax somewhat. "My parents stayed together and took care of me—that certainly taught me about love.

"In considering God's love, though, I feel as if I'm looking at only a square inch of an enormous blueprint that goes far beyond what I know. Just checking my news feed sets off a bunch of questions. How do I reconcile God's love with the evil stuff I read? Yet evil is nothing new. Remember how hostile people ran Elijah Beal out of town?"

They talked a long time. How alive and vital Kendra looked as she analyzed what Garrett said, added her own twist, questioned his and Elijah's logic, brought up the sermons she'd heard on the subject.

After flying over primarily rural areas, they were drawing nearer to the eastern urban sprawl, where she needed to give her full attention to flying. Only a few weeks ago, he'd panicked at her every movement. Despite their "adventures" together, he felt no need to grill her—even if he still took his silent-prayer life up several notches.

While she maneuvered Ladyhawk, he prayed the weather would remain stable. He prayed she would use good judgment and the skills she'd mastered so well.

As they prepared for landing, he regretted lining up this coffee date with his parents, who tended to mask their feelings. Yet, how could he have done otherwise? He couldn't wait for them to meet Kendra.

He prayed his parents would see her for the special, special woman she was.

Although conditions looked good, metropolitan airports always presented challenges. Kendra focused on scanning the air and runways, listening to the control tower, checking and rechecking her instruments. Ladyhawk responded in a controlled descent, doing her part to make a clean landing.

"Good girl," Kendra muttered as the plane touched down smoothly. She reduced power and, using her feet, yawed the rudder to the right. Ladyhawk taxied steadily to the parking area, and Kendra felt the *"Yesss!"* she always sensed upon a mission accomplished.

"You're amazing." Garrett's praise both warmed and pained her as she maneuvered the plane into its designated spot.

If only he hadn't lined up this coffee date with his folks. She should meet them eventually, but with this first separation, she couldn't help hoping they had encountered the mother of all traffic jams on the Beltline so she could have Garrett to herself.

When Ladyhawk came to a stop, he reached over and kissed her gently on the cheek. "You aren't going to your execution, you know."

"I know." She tried to smile. "Would you tell your parents I'll come as soon as I can? I want to run my plane checklists and make sure she's refueled so I'll be ready to go." *No more lingering good-byes.*

"Are you sure you can't stay overnight? We could go out to dinner—"

"Please don't tempt me." She'd carved as much time off as possible out of her schedule these past weeks. "I should go to ISU at the crack of dawn tomorrow."

"Of course, you should." He bent until his forehead touched hers. "You don't blame me for trying, do you?"

"I'd be mad if you didn't."

"That's my Kendra." He pushed his door open, pulled his bag from the back, and walked to the terminal.

My Kendra.

She watched every step. Then, as Garrett disappeared into the glass and brick building, she hopped out, turned, and lifted heavy hands to inspect Ladyhawk's wings for the trip back to Indiana.

His mother's patrician blue eyes X-rayed him through designer glasses. "I know you think your eye is much better, but perhaps we'd better have Dr. Klein check it. You don't look as though you've rested much. Are you tired, dear?"

"Yes." He fought, unsuccessfully, to keep annoyance out of his voice. "But I'm fine, just fine."

"Your mother is simply expressing concern for you," his father intervened.

He immediately felt like a rat. "I know you are, Mother. Sorry to be a little on edge."

"I'd hoped this trip would relax you." She patted his hand as it laid on the table.

"In one way, I've never felt so relaxed in my life. In another, I've never felt so excited."

He knew the answer displeased them. Yet how could he pretend his spiritual pilgrimage hadn't shifted his universe? As if the woman he'd met hadn't shaken him?

"I take it that redhead is your new girl?" His dad had spotted Kendra near the entrance, looking lovely despite her fixed good-morning-class smile.

Garrett, in talking to them, had missed her. He jumped and hurried to her.

"Come and have something to eat." He took her hand.

Dad rose, and Mother extended her hand. "You must be Kendra."

"My parents, Vanessa and Anthony Beal." Garrett wished they looked more enthusiastic, but he did appreciate their effortless good manners.

"I'm glad to meet you." Kendra's professor smile had returned. "Thank you for coming to meet us."

Garrett waved to the khaki-clad server, who took her order for Earl Grey and cranberry scones.

"Piloting a plane must be quite challenging." Dad questioned Garrett's stay in Indiana and his quick bond with Kendra, but he appeared to be putting his best foot forward.

"It is a demanding career, but I've wanted to fly since I was a little girl." Kendra's shoulders, tight as a cable, relaxed a little. "I also enjoy teaching my aviation students at Indiana State University."

"I suppose I find that difficult to understand." His mother

barely suppressed a shudder. "I never fly unless I absolutely must."

Garrett wanted to smack his forehead. How could he have forgotten Mother's dislike for flying?

His father diplomatically changed the subject, but he focused on his golf game and that he couldn't wait to hit the green with Garrett Saturday.

Kendra probably never had held a club. She considered TV golf a major snooze. She did ask Dad if he thought Washington's basketball team would go anywhere this season, to which he answered he hadn't a clue, as he didn't follow them.

Their conversations continued to operate like cogs that never met. Garrett's efforts to fix them didn't work.

Mother asked Kendra about her family. Not content with hearing about Chase and her deceased grandparents, his mother probed about her parents, a subject Garrett knew Kendra would as soon forget.

You're hiding something, said Mother's raised eyebrows and tight smile.

My family is my business, said Kendra's raised chin and equally tight smile.

Dad asked about Garrett's vacation, so he tried to shift the conversation to less controversial subjects. Covered bridges did not interest them. Nor did camping, which his mother defined as living more than a mile from a spa.

Mother did wonder if perhaps the next time Garrett took a vacation, he might think twice before roughing it. "Surely you can find some recreation that won't require medical treatment afterward."

Garrett saw Kendra wince. His mother's words did nothing to soothe Kendra's angst about the canoe trip. Or to make Kendra feel warm and fuzzy toward his mother. *I'm fine. Stop blaming yourself.*

Perhaps the sooner he ended this initial encounter, the better. Kendra did it for him. "I'm sorry to have to run, but I'd better take off. I have a great deal of class preparation to do for tomorrow."

Everyone rose too quickly.

"We understand," Garrett's mother said, though he knew she didn't.

Kendra thanked them again for coming and strode away so fast that after his quick see-you-in-a-few-minutes to his parents, he barely caught up with her.

"Sorry that didn't go the best."

She walked faster.

"At Thanksgiving you'll have a chance to really get to know them."

She nodded, but her face said otherwise: *The thought of that warms me all over.* She hurried toward the exit to the airfield.

"Kendra, slow down." He wanted to make her halt and face him. "Talk to me."

She did pause at the door. She turned to him.

The expression of bleak finality on her face stopped his heart.

Good-bye, Garrett. It was wonderful for awhile, but there's no way this will work. The words tried to take flight from her lips, but their weight sank them into her throat.

She marched past a few curious passersby. He pushed past her and stood in front of the exit. "You are not leaving until you talk to me."

Anger helped her find her voice. "You're going to tackle me, haul me back to that table so your parents and I can intimidate each other for another miserable hour?"

"No, but I'll chain myself to Ladyhawk. With that drag factor, you won't get far."

The mental picture of soaring into the blue with him dangling from the landing gear loosened her laughter and her tears. She covered her face, strangling on chuckles and sobs. "Garrett, I—I wish I'd never met you!"

He gripped her face in both hands and seized her gaze with ice blue eyes. "Do you really mean that?

Yes, I do. She gritted her teeth.

"No." Why couldn't she say what she meant when she was with him?

Garrett dropped his hands to her shoulders and leaned his forehead against hers. "Then even though we have to separate for a while, don't throw away what we have. What we can have, God willing."

His touch was eroding her resolve. She tried to pull away. He held her fast, and she both slammed him and blessed him for that. "But you saw how hopeless it is. You and your parents come from one solar system; I live in another—"

"Not really. They live in one town. You live in a different one. I'm the bridge that can link both."

She couldn't help raising her eyes.

"I do know something about building bridges, right?"

What a maddening man. A wonderful, incredible, maddening man. Her arms flew around him before she could stop them, and a deep, shuddering breath collapsed her against him. For a few minutes, neither said anything. Fine with her. All she wanted was to feel him hold her, his clean-shaven cheek against her skin, the scent of his designer aftershave mingling with her perfume.

"Then you'll give us a chance, Kendra?"

She couldn't say yes, she couldn't—

"You won't base our future together on a single meeting with my parents in an airport coffee shop, will you?" He drew back and stared her down again. "Does that approach mesh with Bible study and prayer, listening to God, letting Him guide our lives?"

"Okay, okay." Sometimes he sounded so spiritual that it bugged her. But she knew he was right. She pulled away, dug for a tissue from her bag, and mopped her wet, messy face. "All right. I'll give us a chance."

"Well, don't sound so excited about it." Garrett raised and dropped his hands in disgust.

She threw her bag down, plastered him against a wall, and gave him a kiss fully intended to scorch his socks off.

When they both came to, heat transferred from her lips to her cheeks. An elderly man—a Hort Hayworth clone—sat in a nearby chair, chuckling. "You two better get married. You fight way too good to let it go to waste."

The most difficult takeoff she'd ever made, but she and Ladyhawk now floated above the miniature city of Washington, DC. Kendra stayed too busy to think much until she guided Ladyhawk over rural Pennsylvania.

Already she ached for the touch of Garrett's hand, his smile. She missed the I-want-the-last-word banter they shared. A blanket of sadness tried to settle over Kendra, dreary as the mostly bare landscape below her. She considered doing a loop just to get her blood moving. But what fun was a loop when Garrett wasn't sitting next to her, trying to act casual as he gripped his seat as if it were a parachute?

Despite his reservations about her version of adventure, he lived in a world of discovery, constantly searching for truth.

His parents, on the other hand—she'd seen life-size cardboard cutouts with more personality.

"You won't base our future together on a single meeting with my parents, will you?" Garrett's words landed in her mind like flies. As she checked her course again, she tried to shoo them away. *I already said I wouldn't.*

But should she also judge his parents by one brief, awkward downer of a meeting?

Did she want them to hang that photo of her in their minds forever?

No, I don't. I'm sorry, Lord. She hadn't realized she was praying while she was thinking.

Was this what it was like to listen to God?

If so, He obviously wasn't interested in chitchat. God felt very, very close.

"So what do you want me to do, Lord?" Needing to confirm this was real, she spoke out loud. "I don't feel positive about Vanessa and Anthony Beal. I can't change that." She figured she may as well be honest with Him.

One word hit her between the eyes so hard she thought something had smacked and broken her windshield: *pray.*

"Pray? For them?"

The impression, like the direction shown on Ladyhawk's heading indicator, did not change. This is the way you must go. Its take-it-or-leave-it quality raised her hackles a little.

What did she have to lose? *All right, God. I will.*

She could tell Garrett something positive regarding his parents when they talked again.

She could say a short prayer for Vanessa and Anthony each day. No biggie.

Chapter 16

Washington welcomed Garrett home. To his surprise, he welcomed it, too. Upon waking, he already felt his pulse syncing with that of the city. His neat minimalist apartment made it easy to grab whatever he wanted without digging past a dozen teddy bears. He could remain in snooze mode as he ate breakfast rather than force himself awake to exchange pleasantries with nice but nosy ladies.

Incredible cinnamon rolls notwithstanding, he didn't miss Snuggle Bears Inn.

He did long for Kendra.

Every redheaded woman—and a ton of them lived in Washington—startled him into a smile. He half believed Kendra would meet him outside this restaurant, that she would sneak around some bush in that park to surprise him, throwing her head back in that husky, bubbling laugh of hers. As he walked to his office building, none of the jets overhead sounded anything like Ladyhawk, yet their whine-roar drew his eyes to the sky as if he would find her there.

You've got it bad, Beal. He grinned. He ached. He sent Kendra another text, wishing hugs and kisses sent through his phone could feel like the real thing.

He trudged through the door, past the pedestal fountain and shiny, bare lobby to the elevator, where vaguely familiar people who rode with him watched floor numbers light up, too. He couldn't wait to get off and head for his office.

"Hey, Garrett." Linc, who worked in the cubicle next to him, slapped him on the back. "What happened to your eye?"

"Wiped out in a canoe." He really preferred not to remember that part of his trip.

"Glad you survived life in the cornfields. But no overalls? No straw hat? I'm disappointed."

"I'll bring your hat tomorrow." Garrett lightly punched Linc's arm.

"We can wear them to the gym when we work out on Thursday."

Welcomes from his other coworkers helped fill some of the vacancy inside him, and his boss, Mr. Branson, seemed excited at his return. Digging through piles of accumulated work absorbed him, blunting the sharp edges of missing Kendra.

Arriving for a departmental meeting, however, he found himself daydreaming about her until Mr. Branson's precise tones woke him to the opening of their session around the big table. Garrett mentally readied himself for his report while various coworkers presented theirs. Projects seemed to be progressing, with only one overbudget problem to discuss. His thoughts wandered daringly to Kendra again until an unfamiliar female voice caught his attention.

Sweet, yet businesslike, it belonged to a small woman who sported a trendy, shining, black hairdo and sleek gray suit.

"Caroline Blakely."

Linc's whisper didn't answer Garrett's questions because the red-lipped woman with the striking black eyes wasn't a consultant, as he'd supposed.

In a nearly brilliant presentation, Ms. Blakely was sharing information only Mr. Branson and Garrett should have known.

She was discussing Garrett's project.

"So you're getting used to living without the teddy bears?" Kendra smiled into her cell as she stirred the kettle of corn chowder simmering on her range.

"Much easier than living without you."

Amazing how a few loving words from him shrank the distance between them.

"Wish you could sample this soup with me." She opened the oven and pulled out two fragrant brown loaves. "And this bread."

A groan on the other end. "Hold your cell up to it so I can smell, please."

She laughed. "Only a few more weeks until Thanksgiving. Then I'll bake you a week's worth. Except you'll have to fight Chase off if you want it to last."

"I can't wait."

His eager tone upped her pulse, but she said demurely, "For the bread, Chase, or me?"

"I miss Chase, and homemade bread rates high on my list. But you?" He paused, and she could have sworn the phone warmed against her throat and cheek. "Kendra, you rate off the charts."

"So do you." Since they'd been discussing love in their study of First John, they'd agreed not to use the word thoughtlessly. Kendra sighed. Would she and Garrett ever be ready to say it out loud?

"I've thought up a special surprise for your birthday." His teasing words brought her back from la-la land.

Actually, she'd rather forget her thirty-fifth birthday on November 9, but if he wanted to do something—

"You still there?"

"I'm trying not to think of what you and Chase have cooked up."

"No need to worry." He lowered his voice. "I just want to celebrate you, Kendra. And us."

After their farewell kiss, she downed two glasses of ice water. *Good thing Chase is going with me to Washington. Otherwise, Garrett and I might have to hire a chaperone.*

His mother probably would gladly serve as killjoy.

Negative thoughts again. She shook her head as if trying to fling them from her mind. She prayed for Vanessa and Anthony every day. Bashing them did not make sense.

She realized, with a small shock, that she now referred to them by name rather than The Parents. She'd fervently hoped her prayers would change them. Had prayer changed her? She ladled soup into a bowl and sprinkled it with parmesan, wondering if maybe she was learning to connect with God. She grinned. *I didn't even have to use a GPS.*

She felt almost as if Jesus were sitting in the other rocker, eating supper with her. She remembered her pastor's words that faith did not depend on feelings. Right, but had she ever felt that close to Him before?

"Thanks that the drainage problem and Jeep repairs were much smaller than I expected." The savings made the total in her Ladyhawk fund look almost plausible. "If Terry will just give a little, we may be able to pull this off."

She felt a little ridiculous, talking to God as if He were her business partner, but, then, wasn't He?

"Good morning, Garrett." Caroline flashed the smile that had half the guys in the department drooling.

"Morning, Caroline." He nodded and turned back to his computer.

"Thanks for sending me the new reports on the bridge in Philadelphia. No one else updated me."

He gave Caroline his team-player smile. "You can't do your job without the data you need, right?" *I wouldn't have minded knowing a few things, either—such as why you were hired without my input.*

"Well, I could try to do without the facts, but I don't think I'd want to drive on that bridge." Another toothpaste-ad smile.

He chuckled politely and waited for her to leave.

She took a step closer. "I see a problem in the numbers for the Hamilton job. Would you mind giving me some suggestions as to how to approach the department?"

Why? You must have had Branson's ear before you reported on my *project.* Smiling, he turned back to his desk. "I'm sure they'll be glad to listen, but if you have questions, e-mail them to me, and I'll do my best to answer."

"Thanks so much." She sounded genuinely relieved.

He immediately felt like a heel.

Caroline left, heads turning as she walked back to her cubicle.

Garrett didn't like the carping, ungenerous voice in his ear.

But he didn't like the artificial apology Branson extended after that shocking first meeting, either. The timing of Caroline's arrival bothered him. Why did she start her job immediately after he left for Indiana?

Could he be training his replacement?

Garrett gulped his coffee, forgetting the new machine practically boiled it. *Gaaa!* He dashed for the watercooler and poured a cupful down his throat, nursing his sore mouth as well as his sore ego.

Returning to his desk, he reminded himself that, actually, this situation could work out well. Branson probably would be promoted next spring. For years, Garrett had worked hard, earning excellent evaluations, aiming at taking Branson's place as head of engineering.

Or did his boss intend to promote Caroline instead?

The beautiful birthday card Garrett sent to her office lifted Kendra's spirits after a draining day. But he'd designed a treasure hunt for her using GPS coordinates.

Ack. I feel ready to drop.

She'd do it, of course, but she couldn't help wishing the coordinates would lead straight to her rocking chair at home.

"Garrett created a treasure hunt for you?" her friend Sarah exclaimed during her "Happy birthday!" call. "Oooh! What a guy! God's making up for last year."

Kendra shuddered, remembering that awful birthday. She'd just discovered her soon-to-be-ex-boyfriend's married status.

The contrast energized her. Run after Garrett's GPS coordinates? She couldn't think of anything she'd rather do.

"Celebrate all the young lives you've helped launch!" read the note on Garrett's card. "Celebrate you!" Below she read a set of coordinates: 39°27′05″N 87°18′27″W.

"Happy birthday, Professor Atkinson." Natalie, Kendra's student, poked her nose in the door. "Do you have special plans?"

Kendra waved her card. "Garrett sent me GPS coordinates. I think they lead me to his gift."

"Love it!" Natalie fixed envious eyes on the card. "Older men must think more creatively than college guys."

"Maybe." Kendra grinned, wondering how Garrett would feel about the label "older man."

The coordinates led her to the airport, where, on a hunch, she visited Ladyhawk. Sure enough, an envelope rested on the pilot's seat.

Chase must have helped Garrett with this. She opened the envelope. The note read, "You've made my stomach—er, heart—do loop-the-loops!"

Kendra giggled at the memory of that angry flight. How did they ever stay together?

She fed the coordinates at the bottom, 39°53.1″N 87°12.2″W, into her GPS.

Turkey Run.

She didn't take long to determine the next envelope's location. Though fall foliage had disappeared, the stark, prewinter beauty of Turkey Run's black, bare trees against neon pink sky flooded her senses as she approached nearby Narrows Bridge.

The liquid quiet of Sugar Creek transfused the glory of the heavens into gurgling, softer hues.

Kendra felt like tiptoeing into the bridge's darkness. Fortunately, a white envelope—with their picture on it—had been taped onto a truss near the entrance. She brought it out into what light remained and opened it. One word.

Remember.

She held it to her heart, then to her damp cheek. How could she forget their promises on Narrows Bridge?

Despite his reassurance, the light of her joy flickered. Grandma used to say, "Out of sight, out of mind." Would her relationship with Garrett continue to span the distance? Their differences? His parents' attitudes?

She glanced at the date the bridge was built, 1882. With God's help, couldn't their bond last, too? Kendra bowed her head and prayed.

The cold pulled her back to the Jeep. She held the note under the overhead light. More GPS coordinates at the bottom. These, however, did not match any landmark they'd visited. They pointed to a spot near Marshall, a few miles away.

How on earth would she find whatever Garrett had planned, especially in the growing twilight?

She needn't have worried. Fluorescent balloons, each bearing a letter from her name, bobbed from a farm's mailbox just outside of town. She turned into the driveway, only half surprised to see Chase waving at her in the semidarkness, his cell clasped to his ear.

She parked. Chase opened her door. "Happy birthday, Sis."

She hugged him. "Thanks so much, Chase."

"I'm just the messenger. You want to talk to the guy who dreamed everything up." Grinning, he handed her the phone.

"Happy birthday, Kendra."

Garrett's voice almost burst her heart. "You're amazing. You know that?"

"Of course. Otherwise, I'd never try to win a woman as wonderful as you."

She melted into mush. "Garrett Beal, sometimes I don't know what to say—"

"You probably shouldn't waste time talking. You have one more message to find."

"Oh really?" She stuck her hands on her hips. "Where am I supposed to look? In the chicken coop?"

"You're close. Try the pigeons."

"Pigeons?"

Chase flashed a light on a nearby wooden sign that read Lorrimer's Racing Pigeons.

Of all the birthday possibilities she'd listed on her mental scratch pad, this fell somewhere near number ten million. Garrett bought her a *pigeon*?

"Come on, Kendra." Chase took her arm and walked her to the lighted barn. "We wouldn't want to keep your feathered friend waiting."

A man with a weather-beaten face opened the barn door. "Come in. First, I think these are for you."

He handed her a gorgeous bouquet of peach-colored roses, whose fragrance outshouted the barn's.

"Thank you." She buried her face in them and then spoke into the cell. "Thank you for the roses, Garrett."

"I wish I could hand them to you in person." The longing in his voice answered hers.

"I baked you a big birthday cookie." Chase showed her a Frisbee-sized chocolate chip cookie with "Happy Birthday" outlined in pink icing. "If you can't eat it all, I'm available to help."

"Of course, you are." She hugged him, laughing.

"But that's not all." The farmer held up a cage. "Gray Angel's waitin' for you."

A plump gray and white bird in the cage uttered its rolling, cooing call.

"Angel flew a hundred miles to bring you this message." The man opened the cage and took the bird out with a practiced hand.

"Message?" She stared stupidly.

"Yep, right here." He removed a small cylinder from the pigeon's leg. "Gray Angel and five other pigeons all flew a total of about six hundred miles from Washington, DC, to bring you this." He handed Kendra a tiny, rolled-up paper.

"Oh Garrett." She'd almost forgotten she still held Chase's cell to her ear.

"Have you read it yet?" His eager, boyish tone nearly squeezed her heart in two.

"No, I'll read it now." She carefully unrolled the note.

Kendra,
You are my treasure. I thank God that He created you, that He made you the incredible woman you are. I pray He will help you soar this year and discover skies you didn't know existed—and that by your next birthday, we will fly together always.

Garrett

Chapter 17

Garrett couldn't wait any longer. Ladyhawk had landed, with his Kendra on her way to the hangar, so he dashed out and met her, pulling her close for the kiss he'd been dreaming of for weeks.

Her lips tasted even sweeter than he'd remembered. "It's been so, so long."

"I've missed you." She leaned her soft face against his. Her light but spicy perfume wafted across his face, drawing his lips to hers again—

"Guys. Guys? I'm a little hungry."

Garrett made himself draw back. A fresh flush of heat crossed his face. "Um, sorry, Chase."

"No, you aren't." Chase grinned.

Kendra's cheeks looked as if they'd burst into flame. "You guys go on to the hangar. I'll secure the plane."

Now that she'd arrived, Garrett could hardly stand to leave her that long. But she needed to take care of business, and he wanted to welcome Chase.

He fell into step with his friend. "Most of our intern interviewees don't arrive on a chartered flight."

"Not everybody has a cool sister like mine."

"True." Garrett let his gaze wander to Ladyhawk then brought it back to Chase. "How do you feel about the interview tomorrow afternoon?"

"Good. I've prepared, and I'm excited to experience your company firsthand."

"You'll wow everybody." Garrett slapped him on the back.

"If I do, it will be because of your help." Chase gave him a grateful look.

"Let's not discuss work too much. I hope we can have fun while you're here."

"Now you're talking." Chase knocked knuckles with him. "I'm looking forward to Thanksgiving dinner with all of us. A couple of friends from Rose-Hulman are going to grad school here, and I want to see Washington with them, too." He turned to watch as his sister, after rechecking the cockpit, exited the plane again. "She's really, really glad to see you."

"I think you know I'm glad to see her."

"Kendra's extra happy today because of another reason," Chase teased.

"What could make her happier than me?" Garrett kidded. Sort of.

"Ask her."

The subject of their banter entered the hangar, dark eyes sparkling, tendrils of long, burnished hair curling around her face, cheeks rosy with the cold. Garrett thought he'd never seen anything so beautiful.

He made himself pay attention as he fought traffic, and he enjoyed catching up during their dinner together at his favorite Italian place. Nevertheless, he blessed Chase when he claimed he'd hung with old people enough and wanted to meet his buds at a nearby Starbucks.

"Don't forget I'll be home early." Chase eyed them sternly

as they dropped him off. "I have an interview tomorrow, remember?"

Probably needed that. Garrett grinned ruefully as he unlocked his door. Aloud, he said, "I hope you won't be disappointed in my apartment." He flipped the light on. His brown leather living room furniture and neutral walls seemed extra plain as he carried in her and Chase's luggage. "Strictly functional."

"No wonder you didn't like the teddy bears." Her gaze found the kitchen table. "Those roses aren't strictly functional." Kendra bent and reached for one with a loving touch.

"I don't buy myself roses too often." He bent beside her, nuzzling her petal-soft cheek. "Actually, they're yours."

She smiled her thanks, her arm slipping around his waist as she straightened. "Your view isn't strictly functional, either."

"My splurge." He walked her to the large picture window where thousands of city lights twinkled a welcome.

"Amazing," she murmured.

"Washington has its own kind of beauty." He contemplated it with her a moment and then showed her to the guest room. "Chase says he doesn't mind sleeping on the sofa."

"He's really very flexible."

"A great guy." But not quite as awesome as his sister. Garrett brewed cups of tea, pulled the sofa toward the window, and when Kendra returned, drew her down beside him.

They sat, reveling in the luminous panorama. He tried to think of the thousand things he'd wanted to share with her the past weeks, but her nearness messed with his mind. So he savored the sweet together silence, the warmth of holding her close, and wondered when he might turn her face to his—

"I did reach a goal this week, one I've been working on for, well, years."

Apparently, Kendra still could think clearly. "And that is?"

The glow of the city reflected in her eyes. "I've worked out a deal with Terry. We're going to sign papers in a couple of weeks, and then Ladyhawk will be mine. All mine!"

She threw her arms around him and kissed him with abandon. Did he mind that he had to share her passion with a plane? Not…so…much…

To Kendra's surprise, no mishaps occurred. The three pumpkin pies and two dozen rolls she baked looked delicious. As they headed for Vanessa and Anthony's home, Kendra breathed a huge sigh of relief.

Thank you, Jesus. Help me bless someone else today.

The minute the thought crossed her mind, she realized she hadn't yet prayed for Garrett's parents.

Lord, please bless Vanessa and Anthony—

"You bless them."

She blinked. The words hung in the air as if someone had spoken aloud.

How on earth could she bless Garrett's parents—other than by not showing up?

She glanced at Garrett. He was focusing on keeping them alive on the freeway. Chase, folded into the back seat, tweeted his friends.

"You bless them."

Her questions grew like flowers in a fast-forward film sequence.

How do I do that? I don't even know them.

Why would they want me *to bless them?*

This doesn't involve praying out loud, does it?

She had no idea what she could offer, when, or how.

But she'd try.

The minute Garrett saw his mother's tight smile, he prayed. Especially when Kendra's professor smile popped up, too.

As he hung up coats, he offered, "Can we give you a hand, Mother?"

"No, everything's fine. The turkey's taking its time, but we'll eat at 5:30, as we always do."

Mother complimented Kendra's bread and pies.

Kendra complimented his parents' Martha Stewart home. Silence.

"If you don't need our help, we'll go say hello to Dad and Grandpa." Garrett steered Kendra and Chase toward the living room.

"And to Uncle Ted." Mother, still smiling, spoke the words through her teeth.

Great-uncle Ted had invited himself? Garrett knew she'd be nervous with Kendra's coming, but his mother's tension levels had read off the charts. No wonder.

Garrett paused at the living room's open french doors. Too late to change their course. He prayed again as they entered.

"Great to see you." His father, looking way too relieved, rose and shook their hands. His hand protectively on her back, Garrett edged Kendra toward the sofa where his two elderly relatives sat. "Kendra, Chase, this is my Grandpa, Irvin Beal. And this"—he shook the white-maned elderly man's hand so he couldn't capture Kendra's—"is my great-uncle, Ted Beal."

"Nice to meet such a lovely young lady and a fine young man, all the way from Indiana." Grandpa extended a pleasant welcome, though Garrett didn't miss the appreciative glance he gave Kendra.

Uncle Ted looked her up and down several times. "Well, boy, you had to go to Indiana to find her, but you finally brought home something better looking than all those skinny girls. Come sit by me, darlin'."

"No, I'll keep her with me." Garrett pretended to laugh, but even as he maneuvered Kendra and Chase to the other sofa, he smelled beer emanating from his great-uncle. Anger, like a flash fire, swept through him. *Did you have to crash our celebration today? You try to pass off your behavior because of your age, but we know better.*

Kendra sat, turned to Uncle Ted and said, "Mr. Beal, are those Air Force pilot wings you're wearing?"

* * *

At first Kendra found it hard to believe Garrett's potbellied, beer-breathing great-uncle had, as a young pilot, flown daring missions over North Korea. As he told of his exploits, however, his knowledge of aviation, though outdated, confirmed he hadn't bought those wings at a flea market.

The elderly man's eyes moistened when he spoke of his squadron. "Best friends I ever had. We put our lives on the line for each other almost every day. Charlie, Eddie, Dick, and Arnold. Neither Charlie nor Arnold made it through the war alive."

Uncle Ted fell silent.

"Felt the same way about my old army buddies." Grandpa pulled an aged leather billfold from his pocket, flipped through pictures, and passed it to Chase. "That's my squad. I'm on the left."

"You look younger than me." Chase sounded as if he couldn't believe it.

Grandpa chuckled ruefully. "I was seventeen. Lied about my age."

"Dinner's ready." Vanessa, her eyebrows raised into her hairline, peered around the corner. She deftly pointed everyone to their places. Though Kendra had enjoyed Uncle Ted's stories, she mentally thanked Vanessa for putting Garrett's placard on her right and Chase's on her left.

After they sat, silence fell—not a comfortable one.

"I suppose," Anthony said, "we should say grace."

"We should." Uncle Ted raised his grizzled chin.

Everyone looked at him as if he'd finally lost it.

"We should," he insisted, thumping the table for emphasis. "I'm glad this pretty young lady here asked me about Korea. Makes me remember. Makes me thankful to be alive."

Silence again.

"Would you say grace?" Anthony looked to his son.

Kendra could tell Garrett was trying to hide his jubilation. "Maybe while I'm at it," he said, "we can pray for our military and their families, especially those who aren't together today."

"Great idea," Grandpa said.

For a moment, Kendra saw the teenager in the worn photo, homesick and afraid, with no faith to reassure him.

She clasped Garrett's and Chase's hands. They, in turn, joined hands with Anthony and Vanessa, and the old soldiers followed suit.

"Father God, giver of life and everything good," Garrett began, "we offer You special thanks today. Thank You for bringing us together to celebrate You and all You have done for us. We pray especially for our men and women in the armed services and for their families, that You would draw them to Yourself and be their help and protection. We thank You that You have given us life eternal with You, if we want it, through Jesus Christ our Lord. Amen."

"Thank you, boy." Uncle Ted nodded. "Now, where's that turkey I've been smellin'?"

Vanessa had cooked a wonderful meal. As everyone complimented her, she relaxed more. When Kendra asked for Vanessa's recipe for stuffed mushrooms, the similarity between her smile and Garrett's startled Kendra.

Anthony asked Chase how his interview went, and her brother charmed the Beals with his intelligence and often funny insights. The elderly men, upon hearing of Garrett's vacation, asked about the covered bridges, and Grandpa even seemed interested in Elijah Beal. Some dinner discussions grew lively, but whenever Uncle Ted's noise level approached the danger point, Kendra asked him an aviation or military question. This tactic also came in handy after dinner during fierce games of checkers between him and Grandpa.

Kendra also managed to talk the elderly men out of arm wrestling for her third pie, splitting it for them to take home instead.

When Garrett hinted at going home, Kendra went to the kitchen to collect the pans she'd used.

Vanessa handed them to her. "Your food was delicious, Kendra. Thanks for helping with Uncle Ted. It made the day much less...complicated."

"You're welcome." Did she detect, for the first time, a little warmth in Garrett's mother's eyes? "Thank you for welcoming my brother and me."

As they drove to Garrett's apartment, she marveled that the day had gone so well. She hadn't done anything spectacular, only offered a listening ear, homemade food, and extra hands to help clean up.

Little blessings.

Hopefully, little blessings that might add up.

The next morning, since Chase already had made plans, Garrett declared a family-free day. "I wondered if we'd survive Thanksgiving," he told Kendra over breakfast, "even before Uncle Ted showed up. I had prayed about it for days." He shook his head. "I guess I didn't expect God to answer."

Kendra hesitated. "I know this sounds weird, but while you were driving us to your folks', He told me not only to pray for them, but to bless them."

He whistled. "That you certainly did. One question from you, and Uncle Ted morphed into a human being—at least, most of the time."

"Had you heard those stories?" Kendra cocked her head.

"A couple, but he opened up about Korea more than I'd ever heard him. Nobody expected him to want to pray." The deep-down warmth Garrett had experienced at the Thanksgiving table returned. "Let's add him to our prayer list. Yesterday was something of a breakthrough for my family. Who would have guessed it could happen through Uncle Ted?"

"Although he did congratulate you twice on dating a woman 'with some meat on her bones.' " She winced. "Almost enough to make me boycott my own pie."

"Almost." He grinned as she swatted him with the rolled-up *Washington Post*. "I think you're wonderful the way you are." He reached over and hugged her. "Now, wonderful lady, where do you want to go today? Maybe the National Air and Space Museum?"

She'd never made time to see it. He loved watching the little-kid wonder on her face as they viewed the Wright 1903 Flyer, Lindbergh's *Spirit of St. Louis*, the Apollo 11 Command Module *Columbia*, and a Lockheed Vega airplane once piloted by Amelia Earhart. She zipped from one exhibit to another, consumed by the museum's magic. Before they returned to Garrett's apartment for takeout Thai and a movie, they visited the newly opened Christmas display at the National Zoo, where colorfully lighted bird and animal shapes greeted them in the winter twilight.

Since Garrett still had not settled on a home church, they dragged Chase out of bed the next morning and attended Sunday services at the Washington National Cathedral. Though aghast at the pinnacles and flying buttresses damaged during the earthquake of 2011, they felt dwarfed by the beauty of its enormous stained glass windows and soaring ceilings, humbled by its solemn liturgies and worshipful music. However, the guest speaker, Tony Campolo, soon had the congregation roaring with laughter. Later, as Garrett and the Atkinsons shared brunch at a restaurant, they talked of little else.

"What a service." Chase finished off another waffle. "If I come to Washington, I want to check out lots of churches."

"You'll find any kind you might imagine," Garrett agreed. "In a way, that makes it difficult to stick with just one."

"But that's important, don't you think?" Kendra set down her cup of chai.

Garrett, cutting his butternut squash lasagna, felt her probing gaze. "I know your family has attended the same church for a hundred years, Kendra. Mine hasn't. I'm still at the exploratory stage."

"Yet a church family makes all the difference in a person's everyday faith. I couldn't have made it without mine when our grandparents died." Kendra wasn't going to let this one go.

"I'll work on it." He meant to do just that.

Right now, though, all Garrett could think was that within an hour or two, he would have to say good-bye to Kendra again and watch Ladyhawk circle high overhead until she disappeared into the clouds.

Kendra dropped her suitcase near her cabin's entrance, headed for the deck doors, and pushed them open, inviting in the dark, soothing silence of the winter forest that snuggled under its first thin blanket of snow. She stepped onto the deck and let the cold breeze freshen her spirit after days of so many people so close together making so much noise.

In one way, the quiet worsened the empty echo of leaving Garrett. In another way, she welcomed it as a healer.

"You're gonna freeze out there," Chase yelled as he built a fire.

Reluctantly she returned, but as Kendra flopped into her rocker with a pile of mail to read, the cheery blaze warmed her chilly toes and made her more thankful than ever to be home.

"Oh, here are the ownership papers from Terry. Already?" Delight filled some of her heart's emptiness. "We'll seal the deal, and I'll finally be Ladyhawk's sole owner."

Chase, not taking his eyes off his phone, gave her a thumbs-up.

She slit the envelope, opened the letter, and began to read. The fire's encouraging light dimmed to nothing.

Terry had decided not to sell.

Chapter 18

How could Terry do this to me? Monday morning, Kendra slammed her briefcase on her office desk, not caring whether her fellow professors or students down the hall heard.

She knew perfectly well why Ladyhawk's co-owner had backed out. Number one: His mother, who cared for his elderly, frail father in Michigan's Upper Peninsula, had just been diagnosed with cancer. He would need to fly there often to care for them. Number two: Because of his parents' limited resources, Terry couldn't afford to sell at the bargain-basement price he'd quoted to Kendra.

She'd raged all night since opening the letter.

She felt like a louse for doing so.

"You can buy a different plane." That's what Chase had said—and essentially what Garrett had said when she called him to report their safe arrival home and cry over the phone.

Number one: She couldn't find a plane like Ladyhawk at a price she could afford. Number two, but really, most important: She didn't want a different plane. She wanted *her* plane. She'd scraped and saved and waited so long....

You know this is my dream, God. Why did You let me hope to own Ladyhawk and then snatch her away?

More work. Garrett tapped a few keys on his computer, then glanced at its calendar. Only a week back at the job, and, like a third grader, he was counting the days until Christmas.

Maybe his increased workload would prove a blessing in disguise. Since Kendra had invaded his apartment with her life, laughter, and banter, he could hardly bear its silent, well-ordered vacuum.

When she'd called from Indiana, weeping and broken, he'd fought the impulse to jump onto a commercial flight and go kiss her tears away—

"Did Mr. Branson brief you on his newest idea?"

Garrett blinked. Caroline paused in his doorway.

"Which one?"

She handed him a folder.

He scanned its first page. "No. Haven't seen this one."

"He wants to meet with us at two today to talk about it."

Why hadn't Branson called him? Or at least, sent an e-mail? He checked his calendar, marked the time, and dropped the folder onto his desk. "Fine. I'll need to review this."

"No problem." Caroline's smile did brighten his gray morning until she said, "I've already looked at it."

Of course, she had.

Making an effort, he returned the smile, spouted a pleasantry, and placed his hands on his keyboard in the universal, polite I'm-very-busy-please-get-lost gesture.

Caroline did, but not before she leaned slightly forward, giving him a view of her smooth, creamy throat, a whiff of her subtle yet intoxicating perfume, plus a slow flick of her long eyelashes.

He sat for some minutes after she left, trying to recover, as if from a collision.

* * *

"Sorry." Natalie corrected her flight position on the Beech-craft King Air simulator.

Kendra, sitting behind her, tried not to roll her eyes. The third mistake Natalie had made this morning. Her top student wouldn't have done this a year ago. Natalie's recent assignments hadn't measured up to her usual excellence, either. What was with her, anyway?

When she finished the flight, Kendra said, "Could you fit in a session next week? The extra practice would prepare you better for your final exam."

To her chagrin, a tear trickled down the girl's cheek. "I–I'm sorry I haven't done well the past couple of weeks. I'll try… my…best… ."

Her last word ended in a choked sob.

Kendra slipped an arm around Natalie's shoulders and quickly walked her out into the hall. "Is there some way I can help you?"

Natalie's shoulders shuddered, but she didn't answer.

"Maybe we can talk in my office?"

Not raising her eyes, the girl slowly nodded.

"I need to touch base with another student here in the lab, but I can meet you up there afterward. Would you like a cup of coffee? Tea?"

Natalie almost whispered, "Coffee, please."

"See you in fifteen minutes." Kendra gave a small wave, spoke with a student flying in the Cessna 172 Skyhawk simulator, and then headed for her office, wondering how she'd entangled herself in this situation.

She helped solve her students' aviation and academic problems, dug up financial resources when their bank balances dwindled, and constantly cheered them on. She had gone beyond the call of duty when two were hospitalized. But something told her Natalie was experiencing deeper problems.

A psychologist she wasn't, especially right now, when she

was messed up about Ladyhawk. Nor had she ever been the mama type.

Yet how could she turn away from those sad eyes? *Lord, I know You and I aren't on the best terms at the moment. But please help me help Natalie.*

Upon entering the department, Kendra collected drinks, took a deep breath, and walked to her office. Natalie lingered outside the door, looking like a lost puppy.

"Have a seat." At least, she'd cleared enough room so visitors could sit. Colorful posters she displayed on the walls and the bright, whimsical pottery she'd scattered among her plants always lifted her spirits. Good thing. She had a feeling she'd need a boost to handle this.

Once they were settled, Kendra said, "All right, Natalie, what's up?"

"Nothing's up." The girl's head dipped. "I'm down. My—my parents are getting a divorce."

At the misery in Natalie's voice, Kendra's heart contracted. "When did you find out about this?"

"They told my brother and me at Thanksgiving." Natalie almost spit out the word. "You know, the time when families are supposed to get together."

Kendra knew nothing she could say would help. She'd felt that sucker punch, too. So she took Natalie's hand and squeezed it.

"Dad said they'd only stayed together for Nick and me. But my brother's a senior in high school now, and I'm in college, so we're old enough for them to split. Old enough?" Bitterness tainted her voice. "As if your kid's turning twenty-one makes it okay to tell her you've been living a lie, pretending to be happy? As if they haven't hurt us? Especially Nick. He has to live every day with this."

Natalie covered her face and wept.

Oh, God, please help Natalie. Her own eyes wet, Kendra slipped her arms around the girl.

Finally, the sobs began to subside. Kendra dug a tissue from the basket on her desk and handed it to her.

Mopping her tears, Natalie said, "Dad moved out before I came back to school. Who knows, by the time I go home again, they'll both be dating." She ground her teeth. "Probably already are."

"Maybe not." Kendra took her hand again. "You're right. This is horrible, and the timing couldn't be worse—holidays, end of the semester—although there's no 'better' time for something so painful. I know. My parents divorced when I was a teen."

Natalie sniffled. "While you lived at home?"

Kendra nodded. "My little brother and I—he wasn't even in school yet—had been living off and on with my grandparents for several years. My folks' final split wasn't a surprise, but that didn't make it any less painful."

"Does it still hurt that bad?"

Kendra's hard-driving, intelligent student sounded like a wounded five-year-old. "Not nearly as much, though sometimes it hurts a lot. Grandma and Grandpa loved us and cared for us. They took us to church, and their faith helped us get through it—"

Natalie gave an angry snort. "My folks go to church every Sunday. They've always dragged Nick and me along. A lot of good that did them—or us."

Better back off that for now. Kendra said, "I just want you to know there is hope, Natalie. Hope for me. Hope for you."

The girl fell silent, picking at her cuticles. Kendra sipped her tepid tea and watched her mobile face, and then the gray December clouds swarming like ghosts outside her office window.

Natalie finally spoke. "May I come and talk when I can't stand it anymore?"

"You don't have to let the pain build to that point." Kendra scrawled her number on a sticky note and handed it to her.

Natalie threw her arms around Kendra. "Thanks. I will."

She gave the girl another hug. Natalie grabbed her backpack and raised her hand in a quick good-bye. Watching the student's small figure disappear down the hall, Kendra prayed for her—and for herself. *Guess I needed a reminder that other people are hurting, too. Thanks, God.*

"This is Richard Branson from Global Working Solutions calling. May I please speak to Chase Atkinson?"

Garrett's company. Kendra's stomach flipped over. "Just a moment, please." Kendra ran the phone outside onto the deck and called to Chase, who was gathering logs from the woodpile. "Phone. Global Working Solutions."

He dropped the wood, dashed to the deck, and grabbed the phone.

She went inside, but hovered near the doors. *Don't spy on him. Don't eavesdrop. You'll find out soon enough.* After she finished loading the dishwasher, she couldn't help creeping closer and closer—

"Thank you for calling. Thanks a *lot*."

He sounds happy. She closed her eyes. *Way too happy.*

"Woooot!" Chase burst through the doors like an ecstatic Irish setter. "I got it! The internship! I'm going to Washington, DC!"

He bounced Kendra around the kitchen so she had to laugh and "Woot!" with him.

Afterward, he called Garrett to celebrate and discuss staying with him during the internship.

She excused herself to the bathroom, buried her face in a thick, soft towel, and cried.

Garrett watched the mole on his boss's cheek wiggle as he talked. Garrett long ago had adopted this strategy for staying awake when Mr. Branson repeated material he'd already heard. Suddenly, though, Garrett's radar zeroed in on what the man was saying.

"How is Caroline doing so far?"

He hadn't expected that. Garrett cleared his throat. "She

does excellent work, cooperates and collaborates well, yet isn't afraid to express a divergent opinion when she considers it necessary."

"Good, good. I'm glad you two are getting along so well." *I didn't say that.*

"You've always done superior work, Garrett. With Caroline's assistance, you've exceeded even our best expectations." *So she's assisting me?* "Thank you, Mr. Branson. I intend to continue that standard of quality." *With or without her.*

At that point, his boss brought up two possible new jobs, asking Garrett's opinions on how to approach them. He felt the old design adrenaline kick in and actually enjoyed the meeting. When Caroline joined them later, she projected her usual charisma, but he didn't sense the suggestive vibes she'd unleashed right after Kendra left. By the end of the meeting, he began to wonder if he'd imagined it. Even if he hadn't, Caroline's behavior could have been only a momentary impulse.

Dinner with his parents that evening went well. His father even asked if he'd like to say grace again. Garrett couldn't remember praying at a meal twice in a row since he was a preschooler. His gratitude welled up freely.

"How's Kendra?" Dad asked.

"She's still upset about her plane deal falling through. Chase coming to DC next semester is tough on her, too, but she's hanging in there."

Mother didn't comment, but her eyes no longer iced over at the mention of Kendra's name. Kendra had tamed Uncle Ted and saved Mother's Thanksgiving dinner from disaster. That feat had earned her forever gratitude.

Just remembering Kendra that day, coppery waves flowing down her back, eyes gleaming like chocolate diamonds as she listened to an old man's stories... He couldn't wait until the meal's end so he could call her.

He headed to his old bedroom after helping Mother clean up, flopped onto the bed, and hit Kendra's number. "Hey."

"Hey, yourself."

Her warm, mellow tone made him wish he could fast-forward the next couple of weeks into minutes. Seconds. "How are things going for you?"

"Classes and lessons are okay. I'm helping a student whose parents just split up. Poor kid's shell-shocked."

"That would do it."

"I'm just trying to get Natalie through this."

"You know where she's coming from." Kendra's compassion for the student only increased his admiration for her.

They laughed, they talked, they dreamed aloud of spending the week after Christmas together, seeing the new year in.

By conversation's end, he felt like running away to Indiana yesterday. "When I come, let's visit a few bridges again so I can collect my rightful tolls."

"Oh really?" That delicious challenge in her voice.

"I hate to tell you, but the tolls might go up. Inflation, you know."

"We'll see about that."

He gave the phone a big *mm–wah* kiss. "I'm at my parents'. I probably should go talk to them some more."

"Yes, you should." She paused. "I'm praying for them. For Uncle Ted. And for Grandpa."

"For me, too?" He knew the answer, but he loved hearing her say it.

Her voice softened. "Seems like I pray for you every waking moment."

"I pray for you, too," he whispered. "Talk to you soon."

"I'll call you tomorrow. Bye."

"Bye." He hung up, deeply satisfied.

And not satisfied at all.

Chapter 19

Having turned in her end-of-semester grades, Kendra slept late.

The aroma of fresh-baked cookies drew her into the kitchen, where Chase, following his holiday tradition, cheerfully destroyed any semblance of order.

With two weeks left before his departure, she wouldn't hassle him.

"Want a Santa? A star?" A photo of Chase's Christmas sugar cookies could have graced a holiday magazine's cover.

"Half a dozen. I deserve them." She poured glasses of milk. They sat and munched.

Will you be here to bake Christmas cookies next year?

Thrusting the thought away, she stood. "Want to find a tree?"

"You're kidding. Don't you want me to clean up the chaos?"

Kendra shrugged. "It won't run away."

"You're abnormally nice these days."

"Don't push it," she retorted. "Especially since I'll soon hold a hatchet in my hand."

"True." He jumped up to don his coat.

Chase usually went along with her preference, but tradition required they wander through the woods, checking out various evergreens before cutting down Kendra's choice. Chase hauled the eight-foot white pine to the cabin. She stoked the fire and set up the tree while he made the kitchen presentable. By evening's end, strings of tiny white lights glowed on the tree's branches. Popcorn and cranberries they'd strung accented Grandma's English ornaments, her quilted "gingerbread" figures, and Kendra's hand-painted wooden ones. Chase polished, filled, and lit Grandma's kerosene lamps. Kendra arranged evergreens on the mantel, the table, and hung their childhood stockings.

She stood back, drinking in Christmas sights and pine-scented smells. "Even better than last year."

"You always say that." Chase slipped his arm around her.

She was right this time. Because Kendra intended to make this Christmas the best ever.

"Garrett, I hear you're headed back to Indiana after Christmas." His coworker, Jermaine, holding his holiday drink, winked at Garrett. "Checking out more bridges?"

"Kendra and I probably will revisit a few."

"Actually, he's doing a special study on curves." Linc elbowed Garrett.

He chuckled and edged away from Linc, who showed signs of too much office party cheer. Making rounds of various groups, Garrett wished them a merry Christmas, gradually edging toward the door. Only a few more—

"Happy holidays, Garrett." Caroline, wearing a red off-the-shoulder dress, blocked his path.

What a knockout. Definitely time to go. "Um, Merry Christmas."

"I hear you're leaving town for the holidays." Her scarlet lips parted in a smile.

"I'm traveling to Indiana again."

"I'm going to New York. Before I leave, though, I want to express my appreciation. You've been key in helping me acclimate to Global Working Solutions. I wanted to give you this." She held out a fancy silver package.

He sucked dry breath.

"Go ahead." Black, velvety eyes held his. "Open it."

Though small, she knew how to block an escape. He couldn't leave without appearing rude.

"Thank you." He untied the black satin ribbon and unwrapped it.

A book. A bestseller in their field. A perfectly acceptable gift from one coworker to another. Relief nearly melted his knees. "Thanks, Caroline. Nice of you to think of me."

"You're welcome." Bestowing another smile, she shifted a hip away from the door, clearing his exit. "Have a good trip."

"Come in out of the cold." Kendra gave Natalie a hug as she entered the cabin. Kendra reached out to the dark-haired teen boy behind her. "You must be Nick."

"Hi." The kid looked as if he'd gladly turn and run.

Chase joined them. "Hey, Nick. I'm Chase. Bring your backpack into my room. Then, you want to grab Christmas cookies and play Wii?"

Nick's face lit up. Kendra thanked the Lord for her brother. When she'd explained the situation, he'd agreed to help. Kendra showed Natalie the futon in her room. "Sorry the upstairs isn't finished yet—it's a mess—or you guys would sleep there."

"This'll be fine." Natalie wandered around the great room while Kendra heated cider. "Your cabin's awesome. I'm sorry we barged in on you two days before Christmas."

"No problem." Kendra offered cookies, but she wanted to smack the young woman's parents. Natalie and Nick had planned to spend Christmas with their dad, but he'd invited his girlfriend to stay, too.

"He just doesn't get it!" Natalie raged.

Their mother was leaving town and "couldn't change" her plans.

What kind of people did this to their children?

Chill, Kendra. Getting mad won't help.

They watched a movie and played games. While the other three were occupied, she called Garrett. "I can't let these kids spend Christmas in that empty house."

"Of course, you can't." Garrett's reassuring voice eased her mind.

"Their mom is supposed to return the same day you fly into Indianapolis—"

"I probably can stay in the teddy bear bridal suite if she doesn't."

"Natalie says they'll go home that day, no matter what. I'll need to check on them—"

"Of course. I want you to myself, but I'll be patient." His voice quieted. "I just want to be with you, Kendra."

"I can't wait to be with you." She grew tired of kissing phones, but she dropped another on hers as she said good-bye.

Unexpected guests, more food to buy, and last-minute presents to buy and wrap.

Less money for her Ladyhawk fund.

Christmas dinner to manage, only a few more days to finish Garrett's gift, and very little time with Chase alone.

Not the perfect Christmas she'd envisioned.

"They're over here, Natalie!" Kendra brandished her snowball. Her student crashed through the underbrush, joining in pursuit of the guys.

Chase and Nick pelted them with snowballs as they dashed away. But Kendra and Natalie cornered them in a thicket and returned fire.

The snow war raged most of Christmas afternoon, and Kendra felt especially glad she'd started round steak with gravy in the slow cooker. With mashed potatoes from a box, it made an easy and filling Christmas dinner. Her guests appeared impressed.

"Someday I'll cook like this," Natalie said.

"Right." Her brother rolled his eyes.

She pretended to swat him.

Their typical sibling behavior warmed Kendra's heart. They seemed to enjoy the time around the tree this morning, too. *Thank You, Lord, for hoodies and gift cards!*

After dinner, the others volunteered to clean up, so Kendra headed to her bedroom to call Garrett. Her cell rang before she closed her door.

"Merry Christmas, Kendra." Garrett's voice made her heart sing.

"Merry Christmas. I hope you're having a good time. We are."

Garrett chuckled. "When Uncle Ted heard you weren't coming, he made dinner plans elsewhere."

She laughed. "Just so you know, you don't have to be jealous of him."

"Whew! That makes me feel better." His voice lost its teasing tone. "This Christmas is so different from last year. I didn't even know Christ. How did I have the gall to try to celebrate Christmas without Him?"

"I don't think Natalie or Nick know Him, either."

"They know you care." His voice softened to a caress.

Saying good-bye didn't feel as painful as usual. Only two more days!

When she reentered the great room, Chase said, "After Christmas dinner, Kendra and I always read the Christmas story from the Bible, just like our grandma and grandpa did. Then we sing 'Silent Night' outside. Okay with you?"

Natalie and Nick exchanged glances, but nodded. They all gathered around the fireplace and Kendra lit the kerosene lamps. Chase read from Luke. "In those days Caesar Augustus issued a decree that a census should be taken of the entire Roman world…."

Thank You, God, for Chase. I'm glad You'll be with him, even if I can't be.

Natalie and Nick, sitting on the sofa, leaned forward, listening.

Afterward they huddled together on the deck as they sang. To Kendra's surprise, Natalie lifted a high, sweet voice, so lovely that after one verse, they stopped to listen as her song traveled past the glittering stars and beyond.

"Your boyfriend's flying into Indy today?" Natalie, stuffing clothes into her backpack, raised her eyebrows at Kendra.

"Yes, around noon." Fireworks went off inside her!

"I hope he realizes how awesome you are." Natalie smiled, but the corners of her mouth quickly flattened. "I might never marry. I'm not too happy with guys right now."

"Not every man is like our dads." Kendra touched her shoulder. "Just like we're not necessarily like our mothers."

Natalie shrugged.

Before they left, Natalie and Nick hugged Kendra and Chase as if they'd been friends forever. Natalie said, "We thought we'd lost Christmas. Thanks for giving it back to us."

"Call soon and tell us how things are going," Kendra said.

"We'll be praying for you," Chase added.

Natalie half-rolled her eyes, but Kendra noticed they looked a little moist.

Later, driving to the Indianapolis airport, Kendra marveled at how much Natalie's words about men sounded so like her own as a young adult. *Unless God works in her life, she won't trust guys.*

A realization startled Kendra so she almost passed her exit. Since her dad left, she hadn't trusted any guy other than Grandpa and Chase.

Until Garrett.

Although, pretending to herself that she was protecting Chase, she'd tried her best to run Garrett off, too.

He'd refused to exit her life.

Instead, his plane soon would land, and she would spend the next week with the most wonderful, trustworthy guy in the world.

Chapter 20

Snowflakes drifted onto the deck, a movie backdrop for the Christmas tree. The fire crackled before Kendra and Garrett, who had pulled her sofa up to its warmth.

Kendra fingered the gorgeous copper and black beaded necklace and earrings Garrett had given her. Could he have picked anything more becoming?

He gave her another surprise. She'd coveted the tiny model of Amelia Earhart's plane at the aviation museum but had chosen to save the money, not realizing Garrett had been watching.

"Of course, I was watching. You don't get away with anything while I'm around," he teased.

She gave him a daring look. "But when you're not around—"

"Then you surprise me by doing something wonderful like this." Garrett ran his fingers carefully over the model of Narrows Bridge Kendra had made. "I knew you did most of the work on this cabin, but I had no idea you liked woodworking, too. My Kendra, the artist."

She kissed him and snuggled contentedly in his arms. A

lazy afternoon stretched before them, even more a gift than the presents.

Chase, hauling his cross-country ski boots, stopped on his way out. "Sure you don't want to go skiing with Natalie and Nick and me?"

"We're sure." Kendra flapped an arm.

Chase shook his head. "Maybe I should stay and keep you company."

"Hey, I'm over twenty-one." Kendra fed Chase his own line.

"Fine." He rolled his eyes. "Just remember, I'm praying for you two."

They laughed as he left.

"That boy will make a great dad someday," Garrett said.

"He was only half kidding." Kendra, suddenly feeling warmer, looked down at her hands.

Garrett raised her chin to look at him. "Chase is right. Staying apart is tough. Being together is tough, too." His fingers tightened around her cheek. "I've missed you so much, Kendra."

"Sometimes I didn't think I could make it another day without seeing you."

His other hand slipped to the small of her back and pressed her to him. "It's so hard to stay within limits—"

"For me, as well as for you." Those gorgeous blue eyes with that glint in them. She didn't dare look into them long.

He nuzzled her nose and kissed her forehead, her cheeks, and claimed her lips... .

Flash fires ripped through her. She drew back, breathless.

He reached for her again—

"Garrett." She edged away. "We want the best for each other, right?"

He gave her such a look of longing that she yearned to give in.

"Right?" she said softly.

"Right." He sighed and fell back against the sofa, hands behind his head, staring at the ceiling.

The longer the silence lasted, the more she felt as if someone had turned a spotlight on them.

So...are we going to sit like this for six straight days, until I fly you back to Washington? She wanted to yell and beat pillows and beat Garrett with them and—

"I love you, Kendra."

Not what she expected to hear. The words sang in her ears, her heart. She opened her mouth to answer his love with hers, then closed it as doubt sliced through her. Surely Garrett wouldn't use those words as a ploy—

"I love you, so I'm going to do my best to follow what the Bible says about sex." He was looking at her now, his jaw set, hands gripped together.

"I love you, too, Garrett." She gripped her hands as well.

Great. Now we'll sit six days straight like this.

"God's take on sex is new to me." Garrett shook his head. "I don't totally understand His logic."

"Even though I've known His way, I didn't always follow it." She felt as if coals had popped out of the fire, onto her face. "But we both want to follow Him, so we can't avoid this subject anymore. We need to help each other." She slowly extended her finger to him.

He hooked it in his and paused. "Is it okay if I hold your hand?"

He looked so disgusted that a giggle burst out of her. His eyebrows shot up, but he chuckled. Soon, both laughed helplessly, coughing and slapping each other on the back.

After they calmed, they poured cider and popped popcorn and spent a long, loving time talking about limits and how they would help each other keep them.

Then they cuddled close by the fire. "Real love isn't easy sometimes," Kendra said.

"Amen to that." Garrett's strong hand found her cheek again, only his touch felt gentle. "But God's other changes in my life have made me come alive. I have to believe this will, too."

* * *

Garrett had never celebrated a New Year's Eve quite like the one at Kendra's church.

"We've put on our talent show ever since I can remember," she told him.

Garrett found himself sitting in a church basement witnessing a spectacle as far from his usual black-tie events as he could have imagined.

A somewhat rowdy but excellent senior tap-dance group and a middle school trio of squeaky clarinets were interwoven among a symphony-level cello solo, cute kid songs, and a tender ballet number performed by a young girl. Two earsplitting teen band numbers and a duet worthy of *American Idol* followed. Then a guy juggled cucumbers.

"Hort could juggle him into the ground," Chase whispered as they applauded. "Come on, guys. Time for the Hallelu Kazoos."

Garrett had thought Chase would change out of the Baby New Year costume he'd worn in answer to his friend's Father Time getup, but he hitched up his large diaper, let his pacifier hang on its ribbon, and waved at his band to gather.

Pulling his kazoo from his pocket, Garrett followed Kendra to the stage. Chase, standing in a choir director's position, turned to the audience. He divided the room in half and gestured. "You guys are the 'hallelus.' " He pointed to the other side. "You guys sing the 'praise ye the Lords.' " The grinning accompanist played the introduction as twenty Hallelu Kazoos raised their instruments.

Somehow Garrett had never considered his Christian experience would include playing a worship song in a kazoo band directed by a six-foot-four, hairy-legged baby.

The pastor's final garden hose solo—he apparently controlled the mastodon-like tone by whipping it round and round his head—seemed like an appropriate finish.

But no.

"Please bring your food for the pantry forward." Pastor Jeff motioned. Like a colony of ants, everyone piled nonperishable items on the platform. The mound grew and grew.

When the last box of macaroni and cheese had been added, the congregation surrounded its offering and joined hands.

"Father, we know you enjoy our fun together and our praise, odd though it may be," the pastor prayed. "We ask that in giving this food, we can share Your joy with the hungry and bless their New Year as You have blessed us. Everyone said—"

"Amen!" chorused his congregation.

The pastor checked his watch. "Five minutes until midnight."

Children carrying baskets of confetti and noise blowers distributed them. Several began to practice blowing them.

Chase turned to Kendra. "I'll take my New Year's hug now so you can concentrate on that guy." He thumbed at Garrett.

"Oh Chase." She hugged him, her eyes squeezed shut.

I'm the one who set his sights away from the Midwest.

Garrett couldn't help feeling a little guilty. But Chase had prayed about his decision for months.

"May the Lord give you a wonderful year, Chase." Kendra dabbed at her face.

"May He bless you with His best, Kendra." He kissed her cheek. "I'll go pour us some punch."

She turned to Garrett. He held out his hands and she grasped them.

"This isn't exactly how I pictured spending New Year's Eve." He grinned.

"With you guys leaving soon, I didn't feel like dressing up and going out. I needed to laugh and get crazy with my church family." She touched his cheek. "I hope you don't mind."

"Hey, now I can say I played with the Hallelu Kazoos." *Not that I'm going tell anybody.* "I pray we laugh together a lot this year."

"Me, too." She leaned against him, and his throat tightened.

Two boys holding stopwatches began to count. "Ten. Nine. Eight."

Garrett and Kendra joined in the chorus. "Seven. Six. Five. Four. Three. Two. One. Happy New Year!"

Pandemonium. Confetti rained on his head. Noisemakers blasted his ears, but Garrett saw only Kendra.

Once his lips touched hers, he wanted their kiss to last forever, but he reminded himself they were at church—sort of— and slowly drew back.

"Happy New Year." Chase handed them plastic cups of red punch. They raised them and drank to each other, then toasted others around them.

Later as he listened to Chase snore in their room, Garrett wondered, with such a funky beginning, what direction his faith journey would take this year.

He prayed Kendra would share every step.

"I thought I'd model your gift." Kendra, wearing black satin pants and a filmy sand-colored top over a tunic, showed off her new necklace and earrings for Garrett, sitting in front of the fireplace. "I love them. Do you think they work?"

He appeared to have lost his voice, so she assumed he did.

He said hoarsely, "Be sure to wear a warm coat—"

"I know. You said we were going outside before we went out to dinner." She donned her boots and coat.

He'd planned this New Year's Day surprise, so she handed him the Jeep's keys. He fingered them as if they were diamonds and drove much better in the snow than she expected. She hoped he didn't think he'd surprise her with their destination. Of course, they were headed toward Narrows Bridge.

A few miles away, though, he turned onto a road she rarely used. He pulled into the circle drive of a farm, and she leaned forward. "Do I hear bells?"

Two glossy black horses shook their bells as a bundled-up farmer harnessed them to an old-fashioned sleigh.

Garrett parked and opened her door. "Your sleigh, ma'am."

She hugged him. "You come up with the most amazing surprises."

"True. Most of them don't involve kazoos."

"You had a good time last night, and you know it."

"Yes, I did." He took her arm, and they walked to the sleigh. "But I hope you don't mind if I'd like a bit more romantic evening with you."

Garrett tucked the thick lap robe around her in the sleigh and talked to the farmer before he took the reins and climbed in.

She couldn't help asking, "Do you know—"

"Though I haven't driven many sleighs, I attended a private school where we learned horsemanship." He guided the sleigh out of the driveway, across meadows, along rarely used roads, gliding smoothly as the horses' bells sang their sweet, wintery song. She snuggled close, inhaling the magical freshness of the snowy scenery, the intense blue sky, the color of Garrett's laughing eyes. A million jewels glittered in the late afternoon sun. She felt as if she might meet Laura Ingalls and Almanzo Wilder in their sleigh any moment.

Garrett pulled up near Narrows Bridge. Jumping out, he tied the horses and covered them with blankets. He helped Kendra out, and they slowly walked to the bridge.

Barely inside, he drew her to him and tilted her face up to meet his.

You didn't wait as long to kiss me this time. The twinge of wickedness she felt melted away within seconds as he pressed his lips on hers, caressed her face, buried his in her hair. She savored his lips, the strength of his arms as he held her, breathed in the clean, strong smell of him, and when he paused, she drew his head to hers and kissed him again.

Finally he said, "You remember the promises we made here, Kendra." His voice was hoarse again.

She took a deep breath. "We promised to one day give our lives to each other."

"Are we ready to do that now?"

She wanted to shout *Yes!*

But—

He looked deep into her eyes. "You don't think so."

She couldn't bear that probing gaze. "Do you?"

"No." He pulled her close and laid his cheek on her head. "Too many unanswered questions."

"Such as 'who moves?' " *If only we could be together more than a few days—*

"We've never dealt with that, have we?"

—And really come to know each other. She said, "I want to enjoy every moment of this last evening with you. I don't want to struggle with difficult issues. Yet maybe over dinner—"

"We can at least address our challenges. Before we go, though, I want to say I believe in us. I want to renew our promises." He sank onto the snowy road. "Kendra, one day, God willing, I will come back to this bridge and ask you to be my wife."

She held his clean-shaven cheeks in her hands. "Someday, God willing, I will say yes."

He rose, and they shared one more yearning kiss before walking back to the sleigh.

"Is there any possibility you would move to DC?" Garrett hated to ask because he already knew the answer.

The restaurant's subdued lights shone on her hair and pendant. Kendra toyed with her fork. "I loved visiting Washington. I loved being with you." She sighed. "But after a few days, I was gasping for air. I hated leaving you, but I couldn't wait to come home. I suppose I could fly elsewhere. I could teach elsewhere. But I'm not sure I could live elsewhere." She cut a piece of meat in her beef burgundy but didn't eat it. "How about you? Would you ever consider moving to Indiana?"

He gulped ice water from his goblet. "I like it here much more than you do Washington. But I've only visited Parke County, not lived here. I love my work, too. Changing jobs isn't easy these days, especially to a less metropolitan area. Besides, I've worked for years for a promotion I'm expecting this spring."

"The promotion's a sure thing?"

He hesitated only a second, although Caroline and her way-too-brilliant smile flashed through his mind. "I think it's highly likely."

Both fell silent as a pianist played mellow music. Kendra had never looked lovelier. Garrett tried not to think of what this evening might have been like if "nos" at Narrows Bridge had been "yeses," how they would be lost in joy and plans for the future... .

"Garrett, do you sense God's direction on these logistical issues?"

He startled. "No. My prayers have centered mainly on us. Our love has grown, Kendra, and we're developing together spiritually."

"True, but will we go anywhere with this if we don't work stuff out?"

He chuckled.

"Did I say something funny?"

"Your questions again. They always send us the right direction."

Her eyes softened, but she stuck to her guns. "So, our prayers will not only focus on us, but also on—"

"My career." He hadn't expected saying it to be so hard.

Kendra struggled, too. "My—my location. That sounds so cold! We're talking about my home here, my cabin, my church, the fields and forests I love, the bridges."

"I like the bridges." He waggled his eyebrows.

Her face colored as she laughed. "I do, too. But let's make sure we have a plan: we both will pray daily about your career and my location."

Garrett nodded. "I feel as if I've been looking at these issues through the wrong lens. Let's ask God to help us see them as He does. Deal?" He stuck his hand out.

"Deal." She took it.

He drew her hand to his lips. "Now, about those bridges..."

"You have a one-track mind."

"No, I don't. I'm all about fireplaces as well. Much more comfortable this time of year."

She gave him a playful, yet smoldering look. "Sounds like a plan to me."

Kendra had witnessed a thousand farewell scenes in airports. She'd considered them a backdrop to her workday.

Her own parting at the small airport in Washington? Not so much.

"Good-bye, Sis. Don't turn my room into a sewing room."

"A *sewing* room?" Kendra laughed and cried into Chase's chest. "Grandma gave up on my learning decades ago."

"I know. That would mean you'd finally gone bonkers."

"Stay out of trouble, okay?" *Thank heaven he's staying with Garrett.*

"I'm always a good boy." Despite his smug tone, Chase's eyes grew wet. "I'll meet you outside, Garrett." He hurried out of the waiting room to the exit.

Kendra's fingertips ran along Garrett's jaw as if memorizing his face. "I've always loved airports, but…" She couldn't stop the tears that rolled down her cheeks.

He held her as if he'd never let her go. "God willing, it won't be long before we won't have to say good-bye."

Later, as she and Ladyhawk soared home to Indiana, she prayed a hundred times it would be so.

Chase had gone to an evening interns' meeting at Global Working Solutions. The kid was doing great, as Garrett had expected. Since they'd been roommates at Kendra's, their adjustment hadn't proved difficult. In fact, Chase had helped to make his return bearable.

Sleet struck Garrett's picture window as if angry. A rotten night to go out. But Garrett didn't want to stay home, either. No fireplace to warm him here.

No Kendra.

She'd started a new semester with a meeting tonight, so he'd have to wait until later to call or Skype. Reading her e-mails or Facebook messages again would only make him miss her more. He opened his fridge, peered in, closed it. He flicked the TV on and off then wandered around the apartment, ending up at the bookcase in his bedroom. He didn't feel like reading, but something educational might focus his thoughts until he called her. He couldn't do nothing.

Garrett spotted the book Caroline had given him. It did cover some of his favorite subjects, so with coffee and the book, he settled into his favorite chair.

He opened it to the frontispiece. A small envelope fell out. He frowned and slit it.

He held an elegant gray card with a phone number embossed in silver.

Chapter 21

"My dad expects me to take care of my little brother *all* the time." The words burst from Keisha, an ISU sophomore. "I'm not his mother!"

"I know how that feels." Kendra leaned across the table, glad their corner of ISU's Commons remained fairly empty. "I was twelve when my little brother was born. My parents appointed me Mom Number Two. For a while, I even served as Mom Number One."

"I like spending time with Nick, but he's a senior in high school." Natalie said. "Big difference."

As they talked and sipped their drinks, Kendra felt as if she relived the days when her father disappeared for weeks at a time, when her mother stayed out all night on weekends. *If only their parents could hear them.*

Keisha had begun to struggle in her aviation studies, as Natalie had, and Kendra had suggested they get together. As the two talked, Kendra occasionally offered a survival tip or teased them to lighten the mood. Mostly she listened and prayed.

Her cell vibrated. *Garrett.* Her heart thumped, yet she rolled her eyes. Silly guy. He knew she was busy. When the evening broke up, with the girls planning to meet again, she called him. He sounded tired and irritable.

"Tough day?"

Pause. "Yeah. Mostly because I miss you so much."

She could forgive that. "Sitting by the fireplace isn't nearly as much fun."

"Glad to hear it." Finally his voice had lightened.

She told him about the students. He told her how Chase impressed everyone.

His report pleased and perturbed her. "Is Chase picking up his clothes?"

A chuckle. "Yes, Mom."

"Tell him he has to clean the bathroom, too."

"Wow, you're bossy."

"You'll be glad I am. Don't let him get away with acting like he's too busy to help." By the time they hung up, Garrett sounded as if whatever had bugged him no longer stuck in his craw. The only problem: after hearing his voice, she lay awake a long time, aching for his touch.

If Mr. Branson could marry Garrett to his work, he would.

Unfortunately, that meant he practically married Garrett to Caroline. Branson and the higher-ups had decided they engineered a winning combination.

Garrett placed Kendra's portrait on his desk and stuck her Narrows Bridge gift in a prominent place in his cubicle, though it didn't fit the contemporary decor. Despite his precautions—or perhaps because of them—Caroline went for the jugular. Workdays since his return had morphed into a nonstop battle.

Not that Caroline dressed provocatively or flirted overtly. She subtly wore him down.

Take that one Friday. After slaving together all week, he caught himself staring at her legs.

She smiled and shifted them for a better view.

Oh God. How can I deal with this?

"Can you do our online Bible study tonight?" Chase asked him at lunch not long afterward.

"No, I have to work late again." He avoided Chase's eyes.

"Man, they are killing you. I thought everyone would dump on me."

"They are working you pretty hard." Garrett knew Chase's direct supervisor had, because of his excellence, given him extra responsibility.

"I love it." Chase said. "After four weeks here, I feel like this is where I fit."

"You think so?" Garrett raised his eyebrows. "After seeing my schedule?"

"The long hours are temporary, aren't they?"

"Probably. I've never had to work this hard before. Branson's making a last push to shine before the company decides whether they'll promote him."

"I'm praying about staying here at Global. I hope they offer me a job." Chase looked serious. "Would you pray, too?"

Garrett's prayer time mostly had degenerated into emergency "Help!" prayers when dealing with Caroline, but he'd gladly throw in a few "helps" for Chase. "Sure."

The unrelenting schedule continued. He grabbed minutes whenever he could to call or Skype Kendra, but they no longer enjoyed those long, thought-provoking conversations. She'd volunteered again to work on the Covered Bridge Festival steering committee, and the group was laying foundations for next fall's festival. She also was flying more commercial trips for financial reasons, as well as helping Nick and Natalie survive their parents' divorce proceedings.

One day Garrett and Caroline fought without a break through a mountain of glitches connected with a bridge in Alabama. It was past five when he caught himself napping, his head on one hand.

"Poor, tired baby." A soft hand caressed his hair, his cheek.

He opened groggy eyes, half expecting Kendra to smile at him. Instead, Caroline's face, only inches from his. Her full red mouth pressed against his, her hand behind his head pulled him close—

"Garrett, could you help me with—?"

Chase's voice shattered into silence.

Garrett pushed Caroline away, only to meet Chase's face, still as stone, before he turned and stalked out of the room.

Kendra hadn't taken Ladyhawk for a goof-off flight in ages. Today she decided to ditch everything and do it.

Oh, the awesome feeling of rising into the air, leaving hassles behind. For some time, Kendra simply flew, hands on Ladyhawk's comforting instruments, thoughts trained only on readings and reactions. She found herself flying in the same area where she'd taken Garrett, Chase, and Hort that angry day.

"Matthew. Mark. Luke. John…" She pulled Ladyhawk into an upward arc and zoomed into a loop, spouting the books of the Bible, laughing at the ridiculousness of it all.

She hadn't escaped anything. Garrett's Sunday phone call had followed her, along with the others these past weeks. She'd tried not to notice the tension in his voice, even as he attempted to tease, the dwindling time they'd spent talking about anything that mattered. No, he hadn't found a home church yet. Could she please cut him some slack about that? His e-mails and Facebook messages lagged in quality and number. They hadn't Skyped since…when?

Even Chase had reneged on their last Skype date. "Sorry, Kendra, no time." His e-mails sounded terse, too.

What was going on at Global? The place was eating her guys alive.

A darker question crawled out of its hiding place. Did Garrett's lack of communication indicate problems involving something else? Or someone else?

"Pray."

She'd prayed, and things had only grown worse. What could more words, spoken or thought, do to keep her world together?

"Pray."

No explanations from God. No guarantees He would do anything.

Again, she flew in blank silence, the clear sky a mockery as thunder crashed and lightning flashed inside her.

"All right." She glared at the peaceful blue expanse. "I know all this is beyond my control. Somehow, I have to believe it's not beyond Yours."

She prayed aloud for Garrett and their future. For Chase and his. For Natalie, Nick and Keisha, and other students she was trying to help. Swooping through the sky, she prayed.

Eventually the gale inside her subsided, leaving her quiet but drained. As Kendra approached the Terre Haute airport, she said, "God, I can't do this alone. Please send me help."

She landed, so weary she could hardly secure Ladyhawk. Dropping into the Jeep's driver's seat, she checked her phone for messages and e-mail.

Nothing from Garrett. Her eyes teared. Nothing from Chase. She longed to call Sarah, but her friend was in Florida celebrating her anniversary.

Wait. An e-mail from Hort. "Red Wonder, you've been on my mind all week. Anything I can do to help?"

"Here's a check for the rest of this month's rent." Chase, who hadn't come home last night, burst into the kitchen and shoved it toward Garrett's plate of canned ravioli. "I'll move my stuff out by the weekend."

"What, you're judge and jury?" Garrett pushed the money aside and stood. "I've been trying to get ahold of you—"

"No need to explain." The young man's eyes bored through him.

"I think there is." Garrett glared back.

"Right. How stupid do you think I am? You think I haven't seen what's been going on?"

Panic erupted in Garrett's gut. What if Chase had been talking to Kendra—

"I haven't said a word to Kendra." Chase read his mind. "I wanted to give you a chance to man up and tell her yourself."

Everything in Garrett wanted to punch the skinny kid, but he gripped the edge of the table. "Could we just sit? God hasn't struck me with lightning. You shouldn't either."

"Oh yeah, bring God into this." Nevertheless, Chase dropped into the chair across from Garrett. "I wouldn't do that, if I were you. He doesn't take too well to hypocrites."

All the fight drained out of Garrett. "I have let Bible study slide. Not much prayer time. I haven't opened Elijah's journal in weeks. And I haven't tried to connect with other Christians—"

"Lately I've felt like I lived here alone," Chase said.

A wave of shame surged through Garrett. Chase was bright and outgoing, but he still was a boy, far away from home for the first time. Garrett leaned his head on his hand. "I'm sorry I haven't been a better friend."

The tense lines in Chase's face relaxed a little. Then his eyes hardened again. "Forget me. Let's talk about Kendra—and Caroline." He almost spat the last name.

"I've been fighting Caroline's advances since I returned after New Year's. Sometimes I've come close to losing. Most of the time I've won." He told Chase about the book with Caroline's number, the relentless campaign she'd waged with subtle gestures and words, and her occasional attempts to trap him.

"I can't avoid her because Branson keeps throwing us together. The past few weeks I've been at war." Relief at voicing his struggle coursed through him, though his stomach still knotted. "I should have asked you to pray for me. But how could I?"

"Yeah, I'm Kendra's brother." Chase's mouth twisted. "Still, I wish you had talked to me. Instead, I stumbled like a fool into your office and found Caroline all over you—"

"She came onto me." What could he do to convince the kid? "I'd fallen asleep at my desk. Actually, I was dreaming about Kendra." He dropped his head into his hands. "I miss her so much I can hardly stand it."

A pause. "I miss her, too."

Silence.

Slowly Garrett raised his head. "I've let my job push Kendra out of my life. Things have to change."

Chase looked at him, unblinking. "So what will that look like?"

"I'm not sure. I'll have to talk to Caroline. And Branson. Soon." He extended a hand to Chase. "Will you pray for me?"

Parke County's Maple Syrup Fair couldn't compare with the Covered Bridge Festival. As far as Kendra was concerned, though, its fun arrival around the first of March couldn't have come at a better time. She needed something to lift her spirits.

Hort thought so, too. "Best pancakes I've tasted in a while." He scraped golden maple syrup from his plate.

"As good as yours?" Kendra plopped beside him at the table, one of many in the fairgrounds building.

"Maybe a little better," he whispered, "but don't tell anybody I said so."

She chuckled. "Nothing like syrup fresh from Parke County's sugar camps."

She glanced around the enormous room. "Tables are filling fast. I'm glad we could eat breakfast together before I join the kitchen crew."

He patted her hand. "I'm glad to see you, Red Wonder."

How she'd needed his grandfatherly presence. "Thanks for coming."

"Where the Lord sends me, I'm happy to go." He rose. "You want more tea? I'm going for coffee."

She nodded and turned her attention to her food. Hort was right. The pancakes were especially delicious. The spicy smell emanating from homemade sausage patties made her mouth water—and reminded her of how Garrett would bypass them in a second. The thought made her so mad she decided to eat seconds. Maybe thirds.

Fortunately Hort returned and kept her laughing with his

homespun stories. Between those and the extra sausage, she felt, by the end of breakfast, that she could survive the day.

"Don't work too hard, Kendra." Hort hugged her. "I'm going down to Bridgeton to visit old friends. See you at the Old Jail Coffee House this evening. We'll sing along with the guitar guys and make trouble, and maybe they'll throw us in jail for real."

She giggled as he waved.

Not just anyone would camp out at Turkey Creek in muddy, unpredictable March—even using Rose and Al's RV. *Thank You, Lord, for someone who cares.*

No one else seemed to. Two skinny e-mails from Garrett the past week. Nothing from Chase. She wouldn't give up on them without a fight. But was she fighting a losing battle?

Hort would counsel her and help prepare for it. She'd call Garrett tomorrow and set up a time when they could talk—really talk. Kendra rose resolutely, gulping a glass of ice water before tying on her apron. Stress always made her hot, but she heard other diners making comments, too. Kendra went to the back door and breathed deeply—although outside, too, felt steamy, not at all like March. *A big-time thunderstorm will hit sometime today.*

The least of her worries.

Garrett slipped into his office early, hoping to collect his thoughts before any confrontations arose.

No luck with that. Caroline waited, looking ladylike in a pearl necklace.

Hopelessness crept up on him, fear he would set himself up to look like a fool.

So what?

"Caroline, we need to talk." He did not sit.

"I always enjoy conversations with you."

Coy words—poisonous, he now realized. "This won't be pleasant." Garrett took a deep breath. "What happened two days ago—or anything resembling it—must never happen again."

She looked at him as if he were remedial. "To what do you refer?"

"You know what I mean."

Shrugging, she leaned back in the chair and crossed her legs. "If you mean one infinitesimal kiss after five o'clock, fine. I wouldn't want to hurt your tender conscience."

"You won't." He kept his eyes on her face. "Please understand, I do not want your attentions."

She said nothing, but her hand fingered her necklace, then moved downward, sliding slowly to her lap.

He looked away. "Keep our relationship professional, please, or I will report you for sexual harassment."

"We'll see who reports whom." Her chair squeaked. He turned. She now sat up straight, black eyes blazing.

"When I return, I want you gone. However, I'll see you here at one to collaborate on this afternoon's agenda." He turned on his heel and left.

Striding down hallways, he felt as if fifty-pound weights had melted away from his ankles. He took a quick walk outside to calm himself. What a feeling, to breathe free air again. Caroline might very well make good on her threat, but he didn't care.

Next stop, Mr. Branson.

"Sit down, Garrett." His boss offered him coffee, putting him on guard. Branson never gave anything without expecting something in return.

"I was just looking over the latest assignment you and Caroline covered. Excellent work."

"Thank you." That went for compliments, too.

"In order to start the next phase, however, I think you should attend this conference in New York." He pushed a brochure across his desk.

"I thought the next phase wouldn't begin until July."

"We had to move it up to cut costs."

Just as you've moved up all the other projects. Reluctantly, Garrett scanned the conference information. "You want me to go in two weeks?"

"You and Caroline, of course."

Praying silently, Garrett braced himself. "Mr. Branson, I will attend the conference. I want to produce the best quality work I can. But I cannot attend with Caroline. I can go, or she can go, but I cannot work with her there. I also ask that our everyday collaboration be restricted to company hours."

"Surely you're not serious." Branson's voice sounded as if he were soothing a recalcitrant child, though his eyes grew colder by the minute.

"I am, Mr. Branson." Garrett took a deep breath. "Despite my refusals, Caroline has continually pushed herself on me through endless innuendos. She gave me her phone number. Recently she tried to kiss me. I told Caroline this morning, once and for all, that I do not welcome her attentions."

The man's eyes froze. "I see." He paused. "Can't the two of you deal with this—"

"I'm afraid not, sir. I'm willing to work professionally with Caroline, but I can do it only under the conditions I described."

Branson stood. His tone knifed through Garrett. "In other words, you insist upon these conditions."

God, please help me. He nodded. "Yes, sir."

Branson stood, walked past Garrett, and faced his window. He said, "I assume you will file a sexual harassment report."

"I consider that a last resort," Garrett said. "I don't want to make trouble. I only want to do my job without undue pressures."

"I will give some thought to the situation." He turned to face Garrett. "As I consider your *requests*"—the man ground the word in his teeth—"you consider whether your personal issues should supersede this company's best interests."

"Yes, Mr. Branson." Garrett looked him in the eye. "I certainly will do that."

* * *

"A good day's work." Caroline gathered her materials, stood, and bent deeply to pack her briefcase.

Garrett turned his head. *No end to your little bag of tricks, is there?*

"See you tomorrow."

Garrett glanced back to see that she'd straightened and then faced her. "No, you won't see me." *No more Saturdays here with you.*

"Surely you don't think we can present this Monday without major work during the weekend." Her lip curled.

"We can work separately and compare notes before the meeting."

She shrugged. "I'll let you tell Branson about your lack of cooperation."

I'll let you tell him why. "Good-bye."

After she flounced out, Garrett tripled his attention on work. He'd put in the hours tonight so he could call Kendra tomorrow. They'd talk all day, if they wanted. Sunday he would go to church and spend quality time praying about his job.

He jumped when his cell rang. "Chase? Oh, sorry!" Garrett shook his head. "I forgot you needed a ride home."

"Yeah, but that's not why I'm calling." The young man's voice trembled. "Tornadoes ripped through Parke County this afternoon. I can't reach Kendra. Not her cell, not Facebook, not e-mail. I don't know where she is. Nobody's answering in Rockville."

Chapter 22

The enormous silence brought Kendra to consciousness, quiet with the life sucked out of it. Something flat and heavy weighed on her.

Lying on soggy ground, she wiggled her toes. Her right knee throbbed. Her head felt as if an anvil rested on it, but she could turn it. When she moved her right arm, pain made her gasp. But her left arm worked fine.

She'd been cooking at the Maple Syrup Fair. Sirens had sounded in nearby Rockville—long, merciless blasts that signified a tornado. People took shelter under tables as a roar shook the entire building. Kendra felt as if someone had thrown her under a train.

She remembered nothing else.

Now she inched her body, trying to slide out from under battered metal siding.

Halfway there. She lay panting then tried again. Kendra freed her upper torso and propped herself up on her good elbow.

She looked around and wanted to crawl back, hide.

Only this morning, people had been eating pancakes, buying maple syrup, and discussing spring planting in that building where she'd served. A monster had bitten half of it off, chewed it, and spat it out all around her. The remaining buildings looked equally wounded. Everything glowed in strange yellow-green light.

Groggy and covered with mud, Kendra tried to edge her legs out, but her painful knee made her clench her teeth. She saw several other scarecrow people rising from the rubble.

When she tried to call to them, everything went black.

Garrett wanted to floor it straight through every state, but made himself stay within yelling distance of speed limits. He skated through the Appalachians while Chase continued efforts to get through. Torrential rains and tornadoes fresh from Indiana stalked them through Ohio. When Chase awoke from a nap to drive his shift, Garrett slept an hour, but the crackling radio kept waking him with imminent threats. He called and checked messages until his fingers ached.

Nothing, nada. Zero.

God, keep Kendra safe. He prayed for the hundreds of people who were suffering such loss. He prayed for rescue workers. But the hum of his car's tires gave their own strange music to his unbroken prayer that stretched from Washington, DC, to Rockville: *Please keep my Kendra safe, oh God. Keep my Kendra safe.*

Where am I? Her eyelids felt as if they were made of steel. This bed seemed hard and narrow. Shifting quilts, she winced. Kendra felt like one big bruise. Something bulky on her leg. Surrounded her right wrist, too. Casts. She'd been injured during a tornado. Scenes with a doctor at the fairgrounds floated through her mind. Did she recall something about horses? Grandma's kerosene lamps?

She hoisted her eyelids open and saw cots covered with quilts. Other people slept. Some wearing bandages and casts, including a few children, sat on the beds or wandered in and out. Stacks of wooden benches lined the walls of the barn-like building. Children's school papers and drawings hung on a bulletin board. Cards with the alphabet and numbers bordered several blackboards. A school. She was beginning to remember. Someone brought her here with other people…last night?

Two women wearing royal blue dresses with black aprons and bonnets entered bearing platters. A flock of children of various sizes trailed after them, carrying baskets and plates.

Amish. She'd been brought to an Amish school. Shadows of the previous night began to make sense. Relief swept over her in waves that quickly ebbed. By now, Garrett and Chase knew about the tornadoes.

The women dished up eggs, biscuits, and gravy. Kendra's stomach growled. How long since those sausage patties?

A rosy-cheeked teen girl brought Kendra a full plate.

"Thank you. Do you know how I can make a phone call? I'm sure my brother is looking for me." *I have to reach Garrett, too. He should know I'm okay, though we're not on the best terms.*

"Even if we owned a phone, I doubt you could call. I've heard the phone lines and cell towers are down. Does he live in Rockville?"

"Washington, DC." Kendra bit her lip.

"Oh my." The girl clicked her tongue. "I'll see if someone can help you."

The food tasted delicious, but Kendra couldn't concentrate on it. *Hort…what happened to Hort?* The girl didn't return. She'd have to find someone. She tried to stand, but her knee made her cry out, and she almost buckled.

Though she sat up, drowsiness, like a thick, warm quilt, wound itself around her. No. No. She didn't want to sleep… .

"Have you heard from Kendra Atkinson?" Garrett asked weary-looking Pastor Jeff. "We went to her cabin. She's not home. She hasn't flown out of the airports. The hospitals don't have her on their patient lists. No news at the police station."

Garrett took a deep breath. "Chase is talking with some of her friends."

The pastor looked as bad as Garrett felt. "I wish I could give you good news." Compassion shone in his bloodshot eyes. "Did you drive all night from Washington, DC?"

Garrett nodded, fear twisting his gut. *How many people were killed in this storm?* He couldn't bear to ask. "I'm just about ready to knock on doors." *Maybe break them down.*

Pastor Jeff sighed. "No one has accurate information yet, but we've set up an emergency center in our fellowship hall. Let's see if anybody knows anything."

They trudged downstairs to where they'd partied in the New Year. People ran in and out in controlled panic, some wearing bandages. Others were giving out or receiving supplies. Two elderly men sat at a table, lists before them.

The pastor greeted them. "Garrett here is trying to find Kendra Atkinson."

The seniors searched their rosters. With each page they turned, Garrett's heart sank lower.

"Not finding her, I'm afraid," one said.

"But our lists are far from complete." The other tried to reassure him.

Garrett covered his face. *Please, God...let Chase find somebody who has seen her. Please...*

A strong hand took his arm and led him to a chair. Pastor Jeff's voice said, "I'll see what I can find out."

Lord God, wherever Kendra is, please be with her. Looking around the room, Garrett saw Kendra sparkle again, as she had at the New Year's Eve party.

He dropped his head and prayed what he didn't want to pray. *I know Kendra's Yours, not mine, God. Do with us what You will.*

Tears ran down his face. He didn't try to hide them.

"Why, Mr. Beal. Are you all right?"

At the familiar voice, Garrett slowly looked up. Miss Esther Kincaid stood before him, every hair in place, which seemed somehow reassuring. Miss Emily stood beside her. Both looked deeply concerned.

He blinked at the paper-doll effect. "I–I'm trying to find someone. Kendra Atkinson."

"Kendra? She's out at one of the Amish schools," Miss Emily said.

Thank You, thank You, God. Garrett leaped up and hugged both ladies. He didn't know how they knew. He didn't care.

Miss Esther patted his shoulder. "Our nephew has been finding out who's where—"

"We wanted to tell the pastor names he'd given us." Miss Emily beamed. "We're so glad we ran into you."

"Thank you, thank you." Garrett wanted to kiss their feet, but he didn't want to listen to them. "I have to go now."

"Good news?" Pastor Jeff at his elbow, smiling.

Garrett told him, and the pastor advised him about avoiding blocked roads.

"I'm supposed to meet Chase here in an hour," Garrett told Pastor Jeff. "If I don't make it back, could you tell him Kendra's all right and that we'll come as soon as we can?"

"Sure. I'll be here."

"God bless you." Garrett ran to his car.

He couldn't reach the school fast enough. When he pulled into the farm's driveway, he practically jumped out before the car stopped. He dashed to the white building's door and threw it open.

People sitting on cots and benches stared at him in unison. They faded to a blur as he saw Kendra before she saw him. Familiar long red hair tumbled down her back, tangled because she hadn't exactly planned a stay in this hotel. Her head was bent, probably reading. After fighting horrible thoughts all day that he should check a morgue, he simply wanted to revel in her safety. *She's been through so much. I don't want to startle her.*

He seemed to walk in slo-mo to her cot. Casts enveloped her wrist and leg, but she was alive. A fresh baptism of gratitude washed through him.

"Kendra."

She raised her head. Her eyes widened. He dropped beside her and took her in his arms.

"Garrett. I wanted you. I wanted you so much," she murmured.

He wanted to hear it a hundred times. A thousand.

Careless of their curious audience, he brushed her lips with his, then claimed them in a long, tender kiss.

Chase leaped from his seat in the fellowship hall as if he had springs instead of feet. She'd never been so glad to see him in her life.

He hugged her. "Kendra! I'm so glad you're alive."

Then he noticed her wrist and leg. His eyes filled. "You're hurt. How bad?"

"I'm okay, but I probably should sit."

Garrett scooted a chair under her. "We'd better take you home."

"Is the cabin okay?" With the bare foundations, roofless buildings, and smashed cars she'd seen during their drive to Rockville, she'd hardly dared believe it.

"Some shingles and downspouts torn off, but basically okay."

She longed for her cabin, her cozy fireplace, her deck. But she'd heard choked voices speaking of missing loved ones and witnessed the terrible tears of someone who had lost a child in the storm.

"Everyone's been so kind. I wish I could do something to help. Maybe I can sit at the table there—"

"Oh no, you don't." Garrett and Chase spoke in unison.

"Go home." Pastor Jeff hugged her. "I wanted to tell you, too, that your friend Horton Hayworth sent a message that he's fine."

Kendra sagged with relief.

"You're going home to rest by the fireplace if I have to chain you there." Garrett sounded like he meant it.

She touched his face. "If you sit by me, you won't have to."

* * *

"You're in Indiana?" Mr. Branson's tone did not bode well.

"Yes, sir." Garrett kept his voice down because Kendra lay asleep by the fireplace. "Tornadoes tore through here. My girlfriend was missing. Her brother, Chase Atkinson—our intern—and I found her, but she's injured."

"I'll talk to Atkinson about how long he can remain. I expect you, however, to return immediately."

Garrett's hackles rose, but he quelled his resentment. "I would appreciate two days—"

"I'm sorry, no."

"I understand." Garrett expected it. After all, the man did have a department to run.

"You're already behind, and you and Caroline have to finish your current projects and prepare for the conference."

Had Branson heard him at all during their last meeting? "Sir, you do recall my requests regarding Caroline? I don't like discussing this over the phone, but I must make sure we're communicating. I am willing to go to the conference, or Caroline can. But I cannot work with her there. Are you mandating that Caroline and I attend together?"

Silence. But only for a moment. "Yes. It's absolutely essential."

"Then, Mr. Branson, I'm sorry. I have no choice but to resign."

Garrett drove Chase to the airport, assuring him he would help Kendra. "Sarah's coming for a couple of days, too, so don't worry."

Chase nodded but said, "I feel bad about leaving my hometown a mess. Rockville and Parke County won't recover for a long time."

"As of yesterday, I'm renting near downtown so I can help at the main shelter. I'll keep you updated." Garrett hesitated. "I hope my blowup with Branson doesn't ruin your chances for a job with Global." He hadn't expected his boss to tell him he may as well stay in Indiana.

"If it doesn't work out, then God has other plans," Chase said. "I'm considering all this a corporate learning experience—something I didn't study in engineering courses."

At the check-in counter, Garrett hugged him. "See you when I return for my stuff."

"Keep praying for me, bro." The young man clasped his hand.

"Pray for me, too." Garrett watched him walk away.

Not only had God led him to Himself and to Kendra, the love of his life, now he, who had never had a brother, felt as if he'd found one.

The late March sun teased Kendra until she had to grade her papers out on the deck. Paella was slow-cooking in the kitchen, sending spicy smells through the screens. Garrett would come for dinner tonight, and they would sit under a stadium blanket at twilight, listening to the frogs' first springtime concerts.

I hope he stays awake long enough to hear them. Garrett had been pouring hours into cleanup efforts. Kendra's casts had limited her movement, but she helped all she could. Their past time together seemed fairy-tale by comparison. But she'd wanted to experience real life with him. That included his snoring through movies and frog concerts.

The crunch of gravel told her he'd arrived. Kendra fluffed her hair over her shoulders and waited for him. Fortunately, real life also included his devastating blue eyes peering at her through his glasses and that smile that stole any complaints she might harbor about his impromptu naps.

He knew where to find her on a day like this. "Hi, beautiful."

She lifted her lips for his kiss.

"Can you take a ride with me?"

"Sure, after I check on dinner."

Riding beside him, she opened her window and let soft air caress her cheeks. "Where are we going?"

"More roads have been cleared around the airport. I thought you'd want to check on Ladyhawk."

Some of the magic drained from the afternoon. "Terry called me. Ladyhawk sustained major damage to her rudder and one wing. Hail dented her all over." She looked out the window. "The insurance payment will cover only a fraction of the repair costs—if they can fix her."

She brushed a tear away and turned to look at him. "Compared to the damage some people have suffered to their lives and homes, it's nothing." She lifted her chin. "I'm not going to fuss. We can go somewhere else."

"Okay." He touched her hair. "Where would you like to go?"

"It doesn't matter."

"Oh, it matters." He turned the Jeep around and drove north.

Her heart missed a beat, but she simply enjoyed the pleasure of watching him drive.

The longer they rode, however, the faster her heart danced.

A little smile curved his lips as he parked close to Narrows Bridge. Garrett said, "How is your knee feeling today? Can you walk a short distance with me?"

"We can do it together." He helped her, and slowly, carefully, they made their way to the bridge. He unfolded a small stool just inside, and she sat.

Kneeling before her, clasping her uninjured hand, he said, "Kendra, we made promises here months ago that we didn't feel ready to keep. Do you believe we are ready now?"

Her heart was doing high jumps. She cupped his warm, intense face in her hand. "Yes."

He shook his head. "I'm not sure about this."

The high jumps halted. "You're not?"

"Well, then I had a well-paying job, financial security." A sly smile crossed his face. "Impressive credentials, if I do say so myself."

"Oh really?" She tried to pull her hand away.

"But if you're willing to take me as I am, by the grace of God, I want to marry you. Kendra, will you marry me?"

He was chuckling now, and though she felt like swatting him, she laughed, too. "None of us are ready but for the grace of God. Sooo maybe…"

She paused so long a flicker of doubt crossed his face.

"Yes!" Kendra yelled.

Her *yeses* echoed through the bridge.

Garrett laughed and slipped an arm around her. "Just because you're wearing casts, don't think you won't pay a major toll for scaring me like that."

"Hey," she answered, "what are kissing bridges for?"

Epilogue

"If men ran weddings, they would look totally different." Chase brushed dirt off his black tux as he and Garrett waited at one end of Narrows Bridge.

Garrett laughed. Laughter came so easily this golden September morning. "I wouldn't mind wearing jeans. Kendra wouldn't disown me. But my mother would."

Chase held up his hand. "I think I hear them."

Sweet, high notes echoed through the bridge. Garrett's heart swelled at the signal. *Finally. I never thought this day would come.* He and Chase walked into its recesses as Natalie sang, a cappella, "For the Beauty of the Earth":

For the beauty of the earth, for the glory of the skies, for the love which from our birth over and around us lies; Lord of all, to Thee we raise this our hymn of grateful praise.

Sarah and Natalie accompanied Kendra as she entered the other end. She wore a simple cream-colored satin dress, a single peach-colored rose in the glorious hair that fell almost to her waist in curls, as he'd asked her to wear it. Her ripe-lipped smile reflected his own happiness. The closer Garrett drew, the more he wondered if he would be able to speak a coherent word.

As they met at the bridge's center, though, she morphed into his Kendra. "Shall we keep the promises we made here?" he asked.

"Oh yeah." Her dark eyes twinkled, a little wickedly, and she grinned.

How could either of them forget his proposal? He kissed her hands and then those warm, sweet lips while Sarah took pictures.

Holding each other's hands, they prayed together quietly. Then they walked to the other end of the bridge, Natalie, Sarah, and Chase following. Hort waited nearby, holding the reins of two shiny chestnut horses harnessed to a buggy. He pumped Garrett's hand and handed him the reins. Hort kissed Kendra. "Blessings on you, Red Wonder. See you at the church."

Garrett and Kendra drove the few miles to the log church through country roads lined with just-turning trees and fields of ripening corn. Kendra exclaimed over bright purple and blue morning glories spiraling up fence posts and cornstalks. They pulled into Turkey Run Park, trotting behind its inn to the forest path they would walk to the log church.

Chase, Hort, and Sarah waited at the small church's open double doors, along with an older woman with short, stylish red hair.

"Hello, Mom." Kendra hugged her.

Her mother held Kendra's face in her hand for a moment, then kissed her cheek. "You are beautiful, Kendra. Thank you for inviting me."

She took Chase's arm, and he guided her to her seat in the front.

Kendra took up a bouquet of peach roses, and she reached for Hort's arm. Garrett kissed Kendra lightly on the cheek. "See you soon."

Inside, Natalie began to sing "Jesu, Joy of Man's Desiring" to a classical guitar. Garrett walked down the aisle, past the rough wooden benches full of family and friends, pausing to hug his mother and dad. Pastor Jeff stood at the front of the church, decorated with flowers and pumpkins. Garrett turned and stood beside him. Chase and Sarah strolled down the aisle next. Chase gave him a discreet thumbs-up as he walked, but Garrett grinned as his soon-to-be-brother's eyes wandered toward Natalie, still singing off to the right.

Now Hort and Kendra, beautiful as the morning, walked to him. In her face he saw the love he'd never thought he'd find, and he thanked God.

Kendra cherished the dress, but after wearing it for hours, she'd had enough. Her feet longed to ditch her heels for comfortable shoes.

The service, in which they vowed their lives to God and each other, had filled her with joy beyond anything she'd imagined. Afterward, she and Garrett had reveled in the happy brunch they'd shared at the Turkey Run Inn with their guests, the fun of feeding each other the rich pumpkin wedding cake and tossing her bouquet and garter—caught, of course, by Natalie and Chase.

The small wedding made it possible for them to chat with their guests. They promised Hort, Rose, and Al to camp with them the next summer.

"Thanks for everything, Hort." Kendra and Garrett joined in a three-way hug with their friend. "You've taught us so much."

Kendra reserved a little time for Uncle Ted, which made him extra happy. They visited with Garrett's parents and Grandpa. Kendra told them, "Thank you for your son."

"You're welcome," was all Vanessa said as she hugged them both. But it was enough.

Garrett had insisted on inviting her mother, and Kendra thanked God for it. They chatted more like acquaintances than mother and daughter, but after all these years, it was a beginning. Garrett and Kendra already had asked her to visit them at Christmas.

Nick, Natalie, Keisha, and other ISU students banged spoons on their water glasses, demanding the bride and groom kiss. Garrett seemed happy to oblige.

They'd laughed and partied, and Kendra had loved every minute. Now, however, she was ready to go.

She whispered to her new husband as they posed for the thousandth picture, "Do you think we might sneak out soon?"

"Sounds great to me." Garrett wore a dangerous grin.

They asked Chase to bring the Jeep around. Kendra and Garrett left in a shower of blessings and birdseed. Kendra didn't peel out as they left the park—she didn't want a sure ticket on her wedding day—but they found a side road where she could throw gravel to her heart's content.

"Won't you get your dress dusty?" Garrett asked.

"Maybe, but I don't intend to wear it again."

They drove to the cabin, changed clothes, grabbed luggage, and jumped back into the Jeep.

"Slow down. Are you trying to get us arrested?" Garrett gripped the seat.

"Sorry."

"No, you aren't." He grinned.

"I just want to run away with you."

No complaints from him anymore.

They drove to Terre Haute International Airport, where Chase met them.

"I wish we could spend more time together before you go back to Washington." Kendra threw her arms around her brother. "Before the wedding, I had a thousand things to do—"

"Don't worry, Sis." He held her close. "You know I'll come home at Thanksgiving."

"You'd better show up to make Christmas cookies."

"You bet. Otherwise, Garrett will have to eat yours."

She swatted his shoulder, her eyes wet. "I love you, Chase. We'll keep praying for you."

"I love you, Kendra. I'm praying for you guys, too." He hugged Garrett. "I know you'll take care of her, bro."

He grimaced. "Yeah, but who will take care of me?"

"Too late for you." Kendra grinned.

After Chase left, she told Garrett, "Just think, you get to fly with me again—that is, if you plan on going on a honeymoon."

"I guess I'd better fly with you."

She led the way to the hangar where Ladyhawk, beautifully restored, waited. As Kendra checked her out, she could hardly believe the difference between the poor, wounded bird she'd mourned and this sleek Ladyhawk, ready for action. Tears threatened and slipped down her cheek. "Thank you, Garrett. Next to you, this is the best wedding gift ever."

He held her close. "Ladyhawk always has belonged to you, Kendra. I'm glad now that she's yours completely. Forever."

She kissed him. Again. Then she admitted, "Well, this isn't getting preflight check done."

"I do want a honeymoon," he said.

Soon they were soaring thousands of feet above the ground.

"Can't make us work today, can they?" He grinned as they passed over Indiana State and Rose-Hulman. Garrett now taught adjunct courses at both schools.

A long autumn orange banner that proclaimed Just Married trailed after Ladyhawk for the world to see as they swooped over Parke County and its thirty-one kissing bridges.

"I've really grown to love Parke County," Garrett said. "Hard to leave for even a little while."

"True." Kendra rechecked her controls. "But God willing, we'll spend plenty of time there together. We can visit the kissing bridges for the rest of our lives."

"Sounds like a tall order." Garrett tugged on his collar with mock angst.

Kendra, watching the sky before her, said, "Consider this honeymoon…practice."

* * * * *

REQUEST YOUR FREE BOOKS!

2 FREE INSPIRATIONAL NOVELS PLUS 2 FREE MYSTERY GIFTS

Love Inspired

YES! Please send me 2 FREE Love Inspired® novels and my 2 FREE mystery gifts (gifts are worth about $10). After receiving them, if I don't wish to receive any more books, I can return the shipping statement marked "cancel." If I don't cancel, I will receive 6 brand-new novels every month and be billed just $4.49 per book in the U.S. or $4.99 per book in Canada. That's a savings of at least 22% off the cover price. It's quite a bargain! Shipping and handling is just 50¢ per book in the U.S. and 75¢ per book in Canada.* I understand that accepting the 2 free books and gifts places me under no obligation to buy anything. I can always return a shipment and cancel at any time. Even if I never buy another book, the two free books and gifts are mine to keep forever. 105/305 IDN FVYV

Name _____ (PLEASE PRINT)

Address _____ Apt. #

City _____ State/Prov. _____ Zip/Postal Code

Signature (if under 18, a parent or guardian must sign)

Mail to the Harlequin® Reader Service:
IN U.S.A.: P.O. Box 1867, Buffalo, NY 14240-1867
IN CANADA: P.O. Box 609, Fort Erie, Ontario L2A 5X3

**Are you a subscriber to Love Inspired books
and want to receive the larger-print edition?
Call 1-800-873-8635 or visit www.ReaderService.com.**

* Terms and prices subject to change without notice. Prices do not include applicable taxes. Sales tax applicable in N.Y. Canadian residents will be charged applicable taxes. Offer not valid in Quebec. This offer is limited to one order per household. Not valid for current subscribers to Love Inspired books. All orders subject to credit approval. Credit or debit balances in a customer's account(s) may be offset by any other outstanding balance owed by or to the customer. Please allow 4 to 6 weeks for delivery. Offer available while quantities last.

Your Privacy—The Harlequin® Reader Service is committed to protecting your privacy. Our Privacy Policy is available online at www.ReaderService.com or upon request from the Harlequin Reader Service.
We make a portion of our mailing list available to reputable third parties that offer products we believe may interest you. If you prefer that we not exchange your name with third parties, or if you wish to clarify or modify your communication preferences, please visit us at www.ReaderService.com/consumerchoice or write to us at Harlequin Reader Service Preference Service, P.O. Box 9062, Buffalo, NY 14269. Include your complete name and address.

LIDIR13